a blue so dark

~

Fifteen-year-old Aura Ambrose is hiding a secret. Her mother, a talented artist and art teacher, is slowly being consumed by schizophrenia, and Aura has been her sole caretaker ever since her dad left them. Convinced that "creative" equals crazy, Aura shuns her own artistic talent. But as her mother sinks deeper into the darkness of mental illness, the hunger for a creative outlet draws Aura toward the depths of her imagination. Just as desperation threatens to swallow her whole, Aura discovers that art, love, and family are profoundly linked—and together may offer an escape from her fears.

More praise for Holly Schindler's

a blue so dark

~

"Schindler's lyrical debut explores the nightmare of mental illness in a voice that is sharp and funny and all her own. This is as real as teen fiction gets. A must-read."

—Crissa-Jean Chappell,
author of *Total Constant Order*

a blue so dark

a blue so dark

Holly Schindler

Woodbury, Minnesota

First Edition
First Printing, 2010

Cover design by Ellen Dahl
Cover photo © Ric Frazier/Photographer's Choice/PunchStock

Flux, an imprint of Llewellyn Worldwide Ltd.

This is a work of fiction. Names, characters, places, and incidents are either the product of the author's imagination or are used fictitiously, and any resemblance to actual persons, living or dead, business establishments, events, or locales is entirely coincidental. Cover model used for illustrative purposes only and may not endorse or represent the book's subject.

Library of Congress Cataloging-in-Publication Data
Schindler, Holly, 1977–
A blue so dark / Holly Schindler.—1st ed.
p. cm.
Summary: As Missouri fifteen-year-old Aura struggles alone to cope with the increasingly severe symptoms of her mother's schizophrenia, she wishes only for a normal life, but fears that her artistic ability and genes will one day result in her own insanity.
ISBN 978-0-7387-1926-9
[1. Schizophrenia—Fiction. 2. Mental illness—Fiction. 3. Mothers and daughters—Fiction. 4. Artists—Fiction. 5. Family problems—Fiction. 6. High schools—Fiction. 7. Schools—Fiction.] I. Title.
PZ7.S34634Blu 2010
[Fic]—dc22

2009031360

Flux
A Division of Llewellyn Worldwide Ltd.
2143 Wooddale Drive
Woodbury, MN 55125-2989
www.fluxnow.com

Printed in the United States of America

Acknowledgments

Heaps, gobs, buckets, mountains, worlds of gratitude to Brian Farrey, who was the first person to fall in love with *A Blue So Dark*, and who has been a terrific editor as well as a fantastic ally and friend to have through the entire book-development process.

Thanks, too, to Rhiannon Ross (for her humor as well as her editorial know-how), to Ellen Dahl (for an absolutely stunning cover), to Sandy Sullivan (for her sharp revision suggestions), to publicist Courtney Kish, to production manager Nanette Stearns, and to the entire—and I really mean entire—crew at Flux, for their unbridled enthusiasm and for making my debut a book I am so, so proud to call my own.

...And to Team Schindler (which consists of my first reader and my greatest cheerleaders)... thank you...

prologue

~

When I was ten, I took my best friend Janny on our family vacation. I really thought we were going someplace special, white sands and blue water, *tropical paradise*, just like Dad told me. "I'll teach you how to swim, Aura," he promised. "I'll show you how magical the ocean is. Someday, you and I will be riding on the backs of dolphins. Surfing off the Baja Peninsula. Snorkeling along the coast of South Africa. It all begins with this trip. *Florida*—a fairy tale drop-kicked into the real world."

But the coastal Florida I saw then, after a string of brutal storms had practically turned the whole ocean upside down and washed every ounce of trash up on the shore, was a freaking lie. Brown seaweed, *that's* what Florida was. Murky, brown, nasty, smelly seaweed. Water that reminded me of the aftermath of floods back home in Missouri, when the lake banks smelled like rotting fish scales and the sour insides of beer cans.

Dad tried—he really did—with his long hair plastered against his forehead and cheeks as he shouted at me, "Kick! Kick, Aura!" But who ever heard of learning to swim in an ocean, anyway, where the tide grabbed you up like a giant's fist while you were trying to get the hang of the stupid breaststroke? No matter how hard I flailed, how hard I fought, the waves kept tossing me aside, pulling me under. And the salt water up my nose didn't make me giggle, like Dad said it would. It just stung.

Dad rented boogie boards, a kayak, a parasail. But I felt like I'd made the journey to the land of fairy tales only to find out that the magical world was identical to the real one. Even in fairy tales, the sun still burns, sand still works its way into your bikini bottoms, and the diner next door to your motel still scorches toast.

I just couldn't get past the thickness of the water along the shore, the sand and the sticks and the dirt that mucked everything up. I wanted an ocean like a swimming pool—I wanted to see my flippers as I tried to tread water. I wanted to see bright-red coral and schools of rainbow-striped fish. I wanted to see ancient shipwrecks, too, their gems and gold coins glittering up from the ocean floor. But when I looked into the water, all I saw was something that reminded me a little of a chocolate milkshake. It scared me, throwing myself into something that I couldn't see the bottom of.

"Who knows what's out there?" I asked Dad. "Maybe jellyfish. Maybe giant fish hooks."

"Janny likes it," Dad tried to tell me, pointing as my best friend raced into the frothy white tide, liking the feel of being knocked over, engulfed. I guessed, for her, it was a little like being on an amusement park ride that didn't have seat belts, or a defined course, or tracks. It was a ride that could take her anywhere.

And, I guess, that was exactly what was terrifying me.

"Yeah, well, there could even be *sharks* out there," I said, loud enough to get Janny's attention, because we'd seen *Jaws* at her house earlier that summer.

"Sharks?" she asked, pulling herself away from the lip of the water. "Sharks?"

That was enough to convince her to mope with me all down the coast—two skinny girls, all kneecaps and elbows, in our matching silver bikinis, dragging the soles of our flip-flops like a couple of old women who were both too arthritic to lift our feet anymore.

Late August had bloomed, like a giant sweaty orange marigold. Janny and I wouldn't have to slide into school desks until after Labor Day, but college had already snagged its students, and late in the afternoons, frat boys liked to clump around beach towels and coolers and surfboards. On a Friday, two beers into their weekend-long good time, they started hollering at me and Janny, teasing us, calling us dykes, lesbos, queers, because we still held hands like a couple of babies.

"*Lesbos*," they said, all singsong, like they thought there was absolutely no way that we'd actually know what it was. Like it was their trashy little inside joke.

I recoiled, red with embarrassment. But Janny—God bless her—she just turned, threw a pit bull of a face toward their blond heads and tanned limbs, and shouted, "Piss off, you dumb fucks."

Poetry.

Mom had seen it all from her chaise, where she'd been drawing in her bathing suit, fingers flying across the thick pages of her sketchbook while her olive-skinned body soaked up the sun like a paper towel could soak up spilled milk. I stared at her, all curvy and fleshy and strong, jealousy and shame opening up in my chest. Because I didn't think I ever would be—strong, you know? Not like Janny. Not like Mom. I hated being such a wuss in front of the people I loved the most.

Back then, Mom could read me, just like the big print in a kid's easy reader. She winked and closed her sketchbook that was never more than an inch from her fingertips, perpetually stained black from her charcoal pencils. Twisted herself out of her chaise and stuck her feet in her sandals.

"Come on," she told me as she pulled a neon *Sunshine State* T-shirt over her head. "I'm throwing you a life preserver."

The rescue was shopping—and I was so glad to get

away from the crummy water, I didn't even care that it was some lousy souvenir shop with painted seashells and shot glasses and plastic flamingos galore. Janny zipped right for a hot pink sequined tank top and a tube of equally obnoxious matching lipstick. Dad started plunking the tips of his fingers against a steel drum in the back, goofing around, acting like he had a clue how to play it, while Janny started to dance, holding her shirt to her chest, begging us all to imagine how pretty she would look in it.

I stood at the counter, watching the man at the register, all gray and scruffy, take a knife to a piece of driftwood.

"You like mermaids?" he asked, staring at me over the top rim of his readers. "I've seen one, you know. A real, live mermaid. You believe me?"

"Might," I said, coolly.

"You might," he laughed as he used his knife to cut the details into her hair. "She twinkled, the mermaid I saw. But not like the light on water, or diamonds, or stars. Ever since that day, I just can't quit carving her likeness. Used to come up with all sorts of different things—fish, cars, palm trees. Now, I just carve *her*, over and over. Can't quit. Think it's because I can never get her quite right. Never can show just how much she sparkled."

He sighed, shaking his head as he tossed the whittled piece of drift into an old galvanized tub on the floor in front of the counter. I followed after it, finding the *whole* tub full of mermaids—some painted, some dotted with glitter, some stained, some (possibly half-finished pieces) left so natural they seemed to have actually washed onto the beach with faces and long flowing hair and scales.

I dug through the lot, picking up each new treasure and turning it over the way I'd imagined, before leaving Missouri, that I'd turn over seashells along the fringes of the exotic Florida shore. *Mermaids $2,* advertised a sign taped to the gray metal tub, and suddenly, I knew exactly what I wanted to take home from our disappointing trip. I was still trying to pick which mermaid I'd buy when a redheaded sea creature with a shiny gold tail was snatched from my hand.

"How much for all of them?" Mom asked, tossing the mermaid back the way a fisherman tossed back a tiny catch that just wasn't enough. Her smiling face glowed from behind the curtain of her long black hair. God, that smile, it had a thousand watts of pride in it, and stretched farther across her cheeks than the grin she'd worn when I'd won Best Painting in the All School Art Exhibition the year before.

"All?" the man at the counter laughed. "Good grief, lady, waddaya want 'em all for?"

"For my daughter," Mom said softly. She looked down at me, her eyes not just glittering, but snapping with fire, like two 4th of July sparklers. "She can't decide which one she wants. I know, because I'd never be able to, either." She ran her finger down the length of my nose, almost like you'd stroke a favorite pet, adding, "We're just alike, me and Aura."

And you know, back then, the idea of that didn't scare the absolute hell out of me.

I

~

Schizophrenia: A psychotic disorder characterized by withdrawal from reality, illogical patterns of thinking, delusions, and hallucinations. See also: Nightmare.

"Pickles," I repeat for the four hundredth time, unscrewing the lid. "Mom, do you want pickles on your sandwich?"

She doesn't answer, so I dip my hand into the cold, yellowy brine, and take a step toward the kitchen table where she sits, staring out across the yard. Her whole body's so stiff and still, she could be one of the mermaids hanging from the kitchen ceiling.

They've been there ever since we got back from our vacation to Florida, the mermaids. Dangling from slender threads of fishing line tied to the eyehooks Mom screwed into the backs of their necks. In the beginning, the long, magnificent, scaly tails of the painted mermaids caught the sun brilliantly. Now, more than five years later, they're all gray, since they're too high up to dust. The heat of the sun that pours through the sliding glass door has cracked their faces. They look exactly like what they are: sad leftovers of a life that no longer exists.

"Mom!" I try again as I pull a dill slice from the jar and wave it in front of her face. I lean so close to her, I can smell the sour skunk of her underarms, see the glitter of oil on her scalp next to the sloppy part in her long black hair. It's not like her to go without showering, especially on a Saturday, when she's got a full day of drawing and painting classes to teach at the art museum.

She turns to me, finally, her frown deepening like I'm being the worst kind of disrespectful. Like I've just told her I have too many back issues of *Teen* magazine to read right now to waste my time going to my father's funeral.

My father—not dead, but not around anymore, either. A man who snipped himself free of his old life, easy as whacking off that decades-old ponytail. He shares a loft now on the opposite end of town with his second wife, Brandi, and their daughter. Grits his teeth through my occasional visits (why do I even bother, I wonder), and prefers to drink hazelnut lattes in place of thinking about his first family, the trial run.

"What's wrong with you?" Mom snaps, pushing my hand away like I've been waving a dead kitten under her nose.

"Mom, it's just a pickle," I insist, hot chills breaking out across my entire body. "For lunch, right?" As I'm staring at her, I remember how I'd sworn, *Sure, Mom, no meds, no more, not ever again. I'll never make you take them.*

Dad had been the one who'd wanted Mom on meds. The one who'd insisted on them after a particularly brutal episode when Mom had run away from home (like an overly emotional little kid) and headed for the Rocky Mountains. He'd been the first one to actually use the word—*anti-psychotic*—even though Mom had begged him not to make her, though she'd sworn that we were really okay, that we didn't have to resort to amber bottles. "Just tell me what's real and what's not," she'd pleaded. "We can manage it just fine on our own."

"Manage?" he'd screamed at her during the flight home from Colorado, anger having officially replaced the fear that had threatened to swallow us both during her two-day disappearance.

I slumped deep in my seat while the passengers in the first three rows closed their magazines and paperbacks, craning their necks. Rows four and five followed, a ripple effect that made it seem like *everyone* in coach was watching. *No movie today—but for your viewing enjoyment, you're just in time to watch a strained marriage crumble into bread crumbs.*

"*Manage?*" Dad had bellowed a second time. "With *what*? Meditation? Holistic medicine? For God's sake, Grace. *You do not have a cold.* You can't fix this thing with some damn herbal tea."

So she took them, each pill an attempt to hang on to someone who was already gone, at least in spirit. She hated it so much that I really believed I was helping her when I dumped those meds long after Dad left in body and belongings, too—after he'd moved out, scrawled a giant cursive *The End* across the life the three of us had shared. I thought—Jesus. Like some dope, I thought I was scoring up a whole slew of brownie points. I thought I was being Mom's friend. *Please don't take them for me, Mom. No, Dad won't have to find out. He's already been gone two years. It's not like he ever once glanced back over his shoulder. I swear I won't tell. I swear I won't ever make you. I love you more than that.*

Now, though, I wish I could take an eraser to my stupid promise. I wish I'd saved some of that Risperdal he'd forced on her, gotten us some *just in case* before she and I flushed it all. Because I get this awful feeling that we're teetering, you know? Like we've been walking along just fine, hand-in-hand on a gorgeous trail lined with wildflowers, only to glance down and—holy shit—our toes are on the edge of a cliff. And our arms are going around like the blades of a couple of windmills as we try to steady ourselves and keep from falling.

Correction: Mom is floundering, and *I'm* trying to pull her back. It's my job, my role: The Savior. Only I don't remember signing up for it.

"Come on," she barks. "We don't have time for this." As if I'm the one that's holding us back. The bitchy side of me wants to bare my own teeth, tell her I've been rushing to the museum once school lets out so that I can eavesdrop on her afternoon classes—that I watch her through the window while I sit under a maple just outside her classroom, looking down only long enough to work the occasional geometry proof. I want to tell her I didn't even get to work last weekend because I spent it sitting in the back of her classroom, analyzing her every move and listening to the drawing-with-the-right-side-of-your-brain lecture I've heard so many times, I can practically lip-synch it:

"Don't get lost in *what* it is," she always tells her students, propping a chair onto a display table. "Don't get frustrated in your first line on the page—of *course* that first line doesn't look like a chair. It won't until you shade it in and get the shadows right. Don't let your idea of what a chair *should* look like dictate what you draw. Draw what you *see*, not what you *think* you see."

But the thing is, there are times that the line between what Mom sees and what she imagines is completely gone. Because Mom's a stark raving lunatic. And that's not some figure of speech, either. No, *my* mom, Grace Ambrose, is a schizo. A real-life crazy woman. The kind of person who used to get locked in the attic. The kind of person that shows up in movies, eyes bugging and hair dancing like currents of electricity, swearing the "voices" told her to whack her father, mailman, lover, etc. into a thousand tiny, bloody pieces of flesh. The kind of person who, in another era, might have volunteered for a lobotomy, because she was so terrified of her own thoughts, she'd jump at the chance to let some whack job of a doctor stick an ice pick up her nose and swing it around in her brain, cutting it in two.

"You're *taking* too long," she says, like I'm the baggage. "It's lunch hour, not summer break."

She pushes her chair away, stumbling, her feet tangling as she tries to stand. I slam the jar of pickles on the table, put my arms out to catch her, but she falls anyway, smacking her knees against the linoleum, hard. "God*damn* it, Aura," she says, pushing me away like I tripped her. Like I'm the reason she's down there on the floor. She won't even take my hand when I offer.

We leave the half-made sandwiches on the counter and pile into our rusted '86 Tempo. She grips the steering wheel so tightly, the bones of her knuckles try to tear through her skin. And she keeps gulping air like she did last winter when she had the flu and was trying to settle her stomach.

"Maybe you should call in sick," I manage to squeak.

"What the hell for?" she asks. When we get to a stoplight, she looks at me with those probing eyes, reading me, but not really like she used to. These days, it's like the words smeared across my face get scrambled. Because what I'm actually thinking and what she sees are two completely different things. "Sick, huh," she growls.

"That's not what I meant," I try. "It's just—" *It's just that there are times, Mom, times that I'm afraid you really* are *getting sick. It's been more than a year now without the meds and sometimes, when I look in your dark eyes, I see waters as muddy as the waves that break on the Florida coast. I see murky depths that could swallow me whole.*

Mom guns the engine at green, and we wind up speeding past the yellow metal sticks (the city's ridiculous idea about what makes great sculpture) piled on the corner to mark the turn-off to the Springfield Art Museum. We're parked and she's stomping toward the entrance before I can even attempt to figure out what to say.

I follow her inside, straight to the classroom, where I take my seat in the back—the same one I've had since I was seven, maybe eight, and started coming with Mom for her lessons. Technically, you're supposed to be eighteen to get into Mom's adult courses. But the faces that usually show up for enrollment are either slathered in preteen volcanic zits or wrinkles so deep, they look ironed in. To keep from feeling like she works in a nursing home, Mom's always made exceptions, rolled her eyes at the rules, allowed anyone in—even the occasional second grader—who cringed at the idea of being in the baby classes where you were shown how to make funny little animals out of squishy balls of clay.

Even so, this class is full of white-hairs; three of the grandmas dote so intensely on the only two young girls in the room (I peg them for middle schoolers) that when the girls' cheeks turn pink, I figure it's caused by the uncomfortable friction of all that damned petting.

I pull out a tattered sketchbook from my sloppy canvas bag, grateful none of the retirees have zeroed in on me, as Mom unrolls a van Gogh poster at the front of the room and tapes it to the blackboard.

"*Bedroom in Arles*," she says, pointing. "It's hard to copy." She pushes her grimy hair from her face, which looks a little like the ash at the bottom of a barbeque without a stitch of makeup. "Hard," she says, as she digs through the pockets of her jeans, "because—because—"

My stomach knots up as she searches for the words. Her eyes zero in on something halfway across the room, and her face scrunches, like she sees something—some phantom that dances as inexplicably as the images that pop up in my dreams. But the thing is, a schizo can't wake up. And as her face gets harder, more pointed, I think I can see it—a distant sharp curve in the road up ahead. I think I can see some outburst—the kind of thing that will send her students scattering off like bees from a hive that's been struck with a baseball bat. Because *that's* what mental illness does. It takes something beautiful and fragile and perfect—like, say, the love between my parents—the kind of love that once had Dad planting pink rose bushes around the entire house (because pink is for joy and admiration ... and grace, jeez, grace, just like Mom's name), and smashes it into a thousand unrecognizable parts. It carves Mom's face into something monstrous. And I'm a damned idiot for thinking we'd be okay without those amber pill bottles.

"... because ..." Mom stammers. "Hard ... hard to copy, because ..."

I start to push myself away from my stool, ready to grab her arm and run.

But I stop short when Mom's fingers finally emerge from her pocket with a ponytail holder, and her face comes back to life, smooths out. "... because the perspective is skewed," she finally finishes, tying her hair back. "The picture frames in van Gogh's painting look like they want to fall off and clatter to the floor. The chair next to the window sort of seems like it's sinking into the wall. The corners don't match up right, either—the room looks more like a trapezoid than it does a rectangle. Everything's tilted just a little too much in the wrong direction.

"When you all start to draw your own *Bedroom in Arles*," she tells her students, which is their cue to open their sketchbooks and pick up their charcoals, "you're going to find yourselves trying to put it the way it *should* be. To draw what you think you *should* see. But you can't, that's not the assignment. Draw what you *see*, not what you *think* you see."

My eyes start to tear up a little, I feel so guilty. Mom was right—I was overreacting. I *am* an overprotective creep.

I gather up my sketchbook—I've got a hundred copies of my own *Bedroom in Arles* by now—and head outside, sit under one of the enormous maples that are turning the red-hot colors of sunset. I've got a few minutes to blow before I'm due at my job—nothing fancy, just an errand-runner for a photographer a couple of blocks from the museum—so I start sketching the small outdoor stage in the park behind the museum, the one with the stone Corinthian columns poking at the sky, the one where Shakespeare in the Park gets performed every July.

The pulse of skateboard wheels pulls my eyes up. At the opposite end of the parking lot, two skaters weave in and out, like they're both moving through some sort of obstacle course marked by invisible cones. One—a gangly thing with a nose like a toucan's beak—pops his board, trying to land on top of one of the park benches. He misses, though, and crashes into a heap on the pavement, shooting out such a frantic slew of *fucks* and *shits* and *goddamns* that the second skater launches into belly laughter.

Suddenly, my stomach bottoms out, like I've just rounded the top curve on a roller coaster track. I know that laughing skater. Jeremy Barnes, who took one of Mom's drawing courses last summer. Jeremy Barnes, whose baggy Bones Bearings T-shirts could never hide the stunning, lanky lines of his body. Jeremy Barnes, who made funky wooden necklaces out of retired, beat-to-shit boards, the wooden geometric shapes hanging on steel cords around his neck. I'd wanted one of those necklaces so bad, my mouth practically watered—I'd spent most of those drawing class periods sketching Jeremy's profile, and imagining what it would be like to wear something against my skin that his fingers had held, crafted, created.

My stupid girly crush must've been so obvious to Mom, because suddenly, she was coming up with projects for everyone to do in pairs, and always putting me and Jeremy together. Only when I got up close to him, he smelled clean and steamy, like a late-June rain. And I was reduced to a ridiculous, blubbering pile of melting Jell-O. Criminy.

Remembering makes my ears burn all over again.

But I can't quit *looking*. Just like it always happens when he's anywhere near me, my eyes are on strings tied to his wrists. I can't pull myself away. Even from here, if I'd never seen him before in my life, I'd be able to tell he's gorgeous, with a beauty mark. So help me, God, a beauty mark. Right there on his upper lip, like in those old pictures of Cindy Crawford. Only it doesn't look stupid, and it doesn't look girly on him. It looks like something I'd like to eat right up.

"*Fuck,*" Jeremy's friend screeches. "Fuck, fuck, fuck," like machine gun spatter. But I can't look at *that* skater—I'm still staring at Jeremy, at his long hair, wondering, *Who even wears long hair anymore?* Except it really is gorgeous. Usually, with old-school, has-been rocker types, they grow their hair out just to let it go all frizzy and scraggly around their shoulders. But his hair is thick and beautiful, and he really, honestly, could be in some sort of shampoo ad, it if weren't such a girly thing to do.

I wrench my eyes away long enough to realize that the boy who's crashed is bleeding. Both his palms are skinned. He almost looks like he's been peeled. And he's pissed—I figure I would be, too, since Jeremy's still cackling so hard he can hardly even breathe.

The bleeder fires off a few more explosive swears as he stomps off. "Fuck you, goddamn. Pussy. Shit. Christ."

Jeremy's laughter dies, gently, like a breeze trickling out from between tree branches. He starts to put his foot on his board, but tosses me a double take. Stares at me while the dancing maple leaves above me scatter a random pattern of light and shadow, warm and cool, across my face.

Instinctively, I turn, expecting to see Janny behind me, because that's where boys look. Or it used to be, anyway—at Janny, my gorgeous best friend, who always knew exactly how to wear her woman's body. Some girls just do, you know. Me—I've always had these ridiculously voluptuous curves like Marilyn Monroe or Jayne Mansfield or any of the other torpedo-boobed pin-up girls from the '50s, but I'm not the kind of girl who likes it when boys whistle and catcall and make lewd remarks about me in the school hallways. Janny, though, she really used to thrive on that crap. So while I was walking around in my oversized hoodies, she was sauntering toward her locker like she was practicing for the day she was going to be a Victoria's Secret runway model. And pretty boys like Jeremy always came flying, like bugs to one of those lit-up back porch zappers.

But Janny's nowhere in sight; she's home, fighting with her parents, like she does pretty much anytime they're all in the same room—and taking care of Ethan, who's about six months old now. I know that technically he's her son, but every time I see them together, I think he really seems more like some kind of weird tumor that travels all over her body—hip, shoulder, lap.

Like I always do when she's not around, I wish I'd sucked up some of her bravado over the years. Wish I could just stick my chest out, flaunt myself coolly, flick a pair of sunglasses up my nose like it's all choreographed. Shoot some clever one-liner like I don't really care what the world thinks of me at all.

The best I can manage is to pretend I don't notice Jeremy—which is like saying I have never once noticed the sky, or the itchy feel of grass against my legs, or the pelt of wind through an open car window. He's something you just *have* to notice—there's no overlooking about it.

I try to act like I'm completely absorbed in my sketch as the skateboard wheels come thumping over the cracks in the sidewalk. I wish the maple I'd chosen wasn't so close to the sidewalk, because then he wouldn't be able to skate straight for me. But he is—and he's skidding to a stop.

I bite my lip, because he's staring down at my stupid sketch. Jeez, it's so embarrassing that he's looking. I know he's going to start laughing at me, too, the same way he laughed at his friend.

I glance up, and oh, God, Jeremy's so gorgeous; he's wearing one of his recycled skateboard necklaces, this one a black and brown wave hanging just below his clavicle, and I practically ache to touch it, because I figure it's warm from his skin. And I'm afraid that with this thought running through my head, I must be just as transparent to him as I was to Mom last summer. He must know I'm practically slobbering all over myself. And I'm so mortified—like some awful girly-girl—I can't think of a single thing to say.

With the flick of the toe of his Adidas, Jeremy pops his board so that I can see the design on it. I realize he's painted the stone stage, too—only his hand-painted scene of the Greek columns is so surprisingly clumsy, it looks like something a six-year-old would have done with his crayons.

"Yours is good," he says, pointing. "Yours were always good." My stomach dips again, like I've been riding on a high-speed elevator that's come to a sudden halt. *He remembers.*

I glance back down at the abstract sketch I'd started

of the stage. My columns look modern, like something an architect invented last year.

"Fix mine, why don't you," he says, dropping the board down onto the wheels and letting it roll toward me.

"What? I—"

"Yeah—take it. Fix it."

I'm flabbergasted, whopper-jawed. Stuff like this just doesn't happen to me. "How do I—"

"I think I know where to find you, Aura," he says with a wink and saunters off down the sidewalk, leaving me there beneath the maple, savoring his lingering steamy scent.

I feel all hot and wobbly inside, and my brain is just a broken piece of driftwood being slammed by the tide. In our pre-Ethan days, guys got thrust on me by Janny—like that moronic soccer player, Adam Riley, the one who used to hang out with Janny's Ace. Guys would flirt with me on assignment. But this was—*What just happened?* I wonder, daydreaming about what it would have been like if Janny'd been here to see it.

As I try to savor my weird, unbalanced feeling—excitement and sweet wonder—I look up at the window and I see my mom. She's at the front of her classroom, writing something on the same blackboard where she taped the print of *Bedroom in Arles.* At first, all I see is the word at the top: *PERSPECTIVE,* all caps, which seems normal enough. But along the side she's also written *PEPPER* and *PET,* which doesn't make any sense at all. Those words have no place up there on that board. I curse the window under my breath for not allowing me to see the looks on her students' faces. And I start to get the hot chills all over my body again.

It's okay, it's fine, it could be anything, you don't know what they've been talking about in there, I try to tell myself, but my heart is on fire.

Mom reaches out—almost as if to erase her words with her finger—but winds up touching them in the same way she would if she were blind and had to rely on a Braille sign to find out which bathroom belonged to the ladies.

She looks through the window, and flashes that *everything's okay* smile she gave me when I got mono from playing retarded make-out games with that douche bag Adam Riley in the ninth grade. The same smile she gave me when Dad had left, and I caught her sitting on the floor of her half-empty closet, hugging one stray loafer to her chest. The same smile she flashed before standing up on her own two feet, wiping the last tear track from her cheek, and saying, "Come on, friend, let's fill in all these empty spaces, you and me."

And just like I have for the past few weeks, I tell myself that everything really is fine.

2

~

Occasionally, family members may reach a point in which they cannot tolerate the odd behavior of the schizophrenic any longer. Often, this leads them to seek help. Other times, it causes said family member to walk away, like the complete raving jerk that she is.

I don't have a clue how to skate (and don't exactly want to look like a moron trying to figure it out on a busy sidewalk at quarter to one on a Saturday afternoon), so I carry the board to Zellers Photography. I told Mom only vague basics about my little cash-basis job, jumping over the name—*Zellers*—like a hopscotch square. Mom isn't even aware that I know about this particular studio, but it's not that hard to figure out, you know? I mean, the owner, Nell, puts twenty-percent-off coupons for senior portraits in the Crestview High newspaper. Zellers Photography, the address right there in black and white. And the way everybody at school talks her up, you'd think the white cursive *Zellers* in the bottom right-hand corner of the senior pics she takes is actually some ultra-chic fashion label. So why wouldn't I be curious?

I'm frozen for a minute on the sidewalk, just beyond the plate glass, because I can see Nell in there, sitting in the front room of the studio with her chin-length white hair and her big, round black glasses. She has a phone to her ear, and she takes off her glasses to put something up to her eye—some magnifying lens or a jeweler's loupe—and she squints at a sheet in her hands. Probably, I think, some negatives.

She hangs up the phone, slips back into her glasses. When she sees me, she throws her chair back so dramatically, it almost looks like a scene from a silent movie. She opens the front door and stares at me, her lips strung about as tight as one of those high wires that acrobats are always swinging off of at the circus. "Kid," she says, "if you don't get the balls to come in soon, I'm going to go nuts."

"Excuse me?"

"Quit hovering," she says, glaring at me like I'm some random teenager who's chasing walk-ins away from her store by doing a bunch of fancy skateboard tricks down her front steps. Like I'm just some troublemaker—*Scat, kid, no handouts for you.*

Her eyes run me over, up and down. Me in my dad's ex-weekend jeans—the ones he used to pad around in every Saturday, with the Metallica patch on the backside—and an oversized hoodie with giant paint splotches, my coarse black hair falling out from a sloppy ponytail. "That's what you wear to work. *After* you don't even bother showing up or calling last weekend," she says, like what I have is some office job, the kind of thing where I need to wear heels and know my Social Security number and be the legal age for official employment. Her eyes are like shish kebab skewers.

"Nell," I say, wounded. Literally *wounded*, as if it's my mother that's getting after me. My voice comes out high-pitched and whiny, like a child's, which I hate.

"*Nell*," she mimics, singsong, like it's a chant we should be jumping rope to. "Don't tell me—you've got problems." She says it kind of snotty, à la some sweatshop owner with a whip. But her lashes fly backward behind her glasses and her eyes dilate, like she's a little afraid there might really be trouble.

"Maybe I do," I snap back, thinking about Mom and the murky tide I'm afraid is trying to roll in.

Nell's chest heaves. She shakes her head, rubs her chin. Her eyes hit the skateboard in my arms with the force of a kick. "What, with a boy?" she taunts me. Which instantly pisses me off. The sweet, unexpected treat of Jeremy's compliment—had he been *flirting* with me?—turns bad. It's a gold ring I've plucked from the sand at the edge of the Florida shore, only to realize it's staining my finger green. Nell's ruined everything, in less than two minutes.

"Forget it," she finally says. "Whatever. I was fifteen once, too. Before the Civil War."

And like that, she's not mad anymore. She's heading back into the studio, and I'm following her, and she's talking like it's business as usual. "Got so much going on, with the show…" she rattles. But that's Nell. She's really one of those type-A personalities, so high-strung that if she were a dog, she'd be one of those little twerpy things that bark at ear-splitting decibels and just don't know when to shut up.

She rushes to her desk, and I stare at her in her plaid slacks and her white blouse with the big open collar, chunky jade necklace at her throat. She's just so incredibly polished. There's nothing about her that looks messy—I can't imagine her ever making a mistake, like dating the wrong guy or taking a wrong turn in traffic or even so much as leaving her umbrella behind in a movie theater. She looks like a perfect piece of Ming Dynasty pottery behind glass. *Don't touch, don't touch, don't get your grimy little hands all over it.*

Her photography studio's in an old brick building, one of those historic downtown sites with so much age that as I make my way inside, I don't feel like my sneakers are flopping against wooden boards, but against decades. The coolest part of Nell's studio is the way she always slaps her newest stuff all over the walls. Last summer, the place was full of brides, the white froth of their meringue-style gowns flowing everywhere. September, it was animals—plain old house cats and mixed-breed mutts caught in such perfect moments, their personalities zinging like lightning bolts across their faces, you'd think they were human. ("People are insane about their pets," Nell had grumbled with a shrug when I'd tried to compliment her shots.)

Today, the studio is full of framed black and whites, the images so old it's like I've stepped into a time warp. Like it's

1969, because here's an old VW bug—the kind with the engine in the *back*—plastered with NOW bumper stickers, and here's a woman (the tag stuck to the glass says it's actually a self-portrait) with long, ironed hair and a skirt so short it barely even covers her belly button. Another photo's a still life, but instead of apples and oranges, it's an assortment of roach clips and political buttons—peace signs and enameled flowers that scream *Stop the War Machine* and *Anti-Draft* and *End Mass Murder in Vietnam!*

"What is all this stuff?" I ask her, pointing.

"Oh, pictures for the show," she sighs. "Trying to decide which ones to use."

"The show?"

"Yeah—you know," she says, waving her hand like it's nothing—like she's just rearranging some old knickknacks. "That First Friday Art Walk business."

"You're going to be in it?"

"Yeah," Nell says, sighing into her chair. "A change of pace from all the family portraits that pay the bills."

"What's the theme?" I ask, trying to make sense of it all.

"Theme," she snorts. "My—life."

This practically lights my freaking hair on fire. My eyes start bouncing through the details in the photos, searching them the way some ransacker would rifle through the contents of somebody's drawers. "Your *life*?" I say, disbelief wracking my voice.

"What?" she laughs. "You don't think an old lady like me ever smoked weed or got arrested at a war protest?" She grins as she twirls a shock of electric-white hair around her finger.

"Who's this?" I ask, my heart knocking on my tonsils as I point at one of the framed photos. But I'm not talking about the younger Nell in the frozen image, wearing a one-piece swimsuit. I'm talking about the girl Nell's hugging—she's twelve, maybe thirteen, with long black hair. They're laughing in the picture, their bodies tangled like they've accidentally fallen onto the beach. Grains of sand dot their thighs. But they look like they're just so absurdly happy, they don't care that they've crumpled into a painful heap, elbows in stomachs, thigh bones crashing together like cymbals.

"My daughter," she says. I know that's what she says. But the words that bounce in my head, up and down like rubber balls, are *your mother.* Because this is her—Grace Ambrose, born April 3, 1970—when she was younger even than I am now. This is my mother, before illness built a nest inside her brain. And this is Nell when she was Grace's mother, when times were still sweet, when no one knew yet that Mom would leave home in a furious rush, barely eighteen, and never speak to Nell again.

"I didn't know you had a daughter," I lie, glancing over my shoulder at the white-haired Nell. The truth is, Nell's the one who doesn't know she has a granddaughter, let alone that her granddaughter is standing in her very own studio, as she has just about every Saturday for the past five months now, because she wanted to know if her grandmother really *was* the evil incarnate her mother always made her out to be.

"Yeah, well, you know—" Nell says, her voice trailing

off like a pop song that fades at the end instead of culminating in one loud, final guitar chord. "It's complicated."

"Mothers are complicated, too," I mumble.

"Yours must be," Nell laughs. "I swear, with a name like 'Aura,' I always figured somebody drop-kicked you in the woods—only, instead of being raised by wolves, you were raised by the last hippie commune on the face of the earth."

Thank God my town is just big enough to get lost in. If I lived in a real-life Mayberry, I'd never be able to pull this off—Nell would have known exactly who I was the minute I'd shown up. Or the town busybody would have grabbed Mom's sleeve in the coffee aisle of the grocery store, blabbing that I was at Nell's studio—and I'd be in the coldest, darkest dog house ever built. I never would have gotten a chance to know my grandmother.

I turn back to the photo that looks exactly like the fairy tale I'd once believed in, back before I'd seen the reality of the ocean. White sands, blue water. Tropical paradise. In a place like this, I'd believe a girl could learn to swim. Here, I'd bet that Nell and Mom really did compete in a surfing competition.

"You remind me of her," Nell says. "My daughter."

I find myself backing away from these words, my sneakers squeaking on the historic floor, the way I'd try to back away from a rabid dog.

"But I can't use that one, anyway," Nell mutters, pointing at the beach picture. "My husband took it, not me."

That makes me work even harder to grab the details

that swirl up at me from the photograph. Chipped toenail polish, soggy strands of hair trailing across a cheek, a dimple, a scab on a knee. *My grandfather took this picture.*

Nell's nervous laughter shakes a little of the seriousness from the room. "All right, kid," she says. "You come to work, or not?"

"Sure," I mumble. "But do I—do I really remind you of your daughter?"

"Every time I see you," she says, the words like bullets ricocheting off the walls.

3

~

Few family members act on warning signs when they first present themselves in a schizophrenic patient. It is often quite hard to realize, in fact, that something is clinically wrong.

If life were a John Hughes movie—*Pretty in Pink, The Breakfast Club,* etc., etc.—the Circle would be the bad-ass place to hang out. The Circle (the weird little cul-de-sac that juts into the field that stands between Crestview High and the Tire & Lube of Kmart) would be where the weirdos, punks, airheads, and druggies all parked their junkyard saves and stood around smoking before school. If life were a John Hughes movie, the "richies" who went to spas before prom season would always get their daddies to buy them school parking permits for the lot closest to the front door, or better yet, permits at the spacious neighboring Gillenwaters tennis courts—after all, they couldn't let their brand new Mitsubishis get door dings.

Sure, there are a few glistening goldens at Crestview—maybe four or five in each class. The ones who really do drive new cars and greet all the teachers by name in the hallways and seem to have the world under their professionally polished artificial thumbnails. But the rest of us are gypsies. And I don't mean that in a romantic, European history way. I mean it in a *lowest of the low* kind of way. A *watch out for that gypsy scum* kind of way. A *you are just a nomad, you will not be in this school forever, and you have no respect for anything in it. You have no respect for yourselves* kind of way.

As I cut across the Kmart lot, I can see that the crowds have already started clustering at the Circle, and yeah, they're smoking, and, okay, some of them look a little rough, and all right, I'll admit, they're all out here because it's technically beyond school grounds and Mr. Groce (sounds like *gross*), the school security guard, can't patrol it. But it's not anarchy, you know? It's just freedom. One last moment to breathe deep before stepping through the door and becoming gypsy tramps.

As soon as the toe of my sneaker touches the Circle, I see him. Jeremy. And goddamn it, my heart flops like a dying fish.

He's standing in a cluster of black T-shirts—together, they look like the wilted petals on a single dead flower. And everyone he's with is smoking, but he's just standing there, hands in his pockets, staring right at me. The wind blows his long brown hair across his face, covering up his beauty mark for a minute.

"You get my board done yet?" he calls out. His words form a speed bump that stretches all the way up to my knees.

I stutter, I stumble, I glance to the opposite side of the Circle, where Janny's leaning against her two-toned p.o.s.—the red compact with blue fenders—smoking a cigarette. I try to telepathically get her to look my way, to *see* what's going on here, because I haven't talked to her all weekend, even though I left a bunch of messages. I haven't gotten a chance to brag about what happened with Jeremy outside the museum … and it would really be so much better if Janny would just look this way and see him hitting on me. I swear, this stuff only happens to girls like Janny, who last fall had practically laughed her panties off when she'd found herself written up on the door of one of the Crestview High bathroom stalls: *Janny Jamison is a SLUT!*

"Look," Janny'd said, proudly. "I'm what you'd get if you'd put Carmen Electra, Pam Anderson, and Kim Kardashian in a blender and pressed *purée.*" She'd taken a pen from her own backpack and scrawled *Jealous! You had to lose your virginity to your own HAND!!!*

I want Janny to see me with Jeremy and flash a *you naughty girl* smile at me, her mischievous eyes bouncing with glitter. I want her to unfasten that old silver bracelet she's always worn and tie her hair back with it—seriously. It was always her favorite thing to do with her hair—to pin her unending piles of unfathomably thick chestnut waves back with her bracelet and walk down the school hallways, with girls pointing and wondering out loud how that was even possible.

But Janny doesn't look up from her cigarette that she flicks, sending ash onto her sneakers. And when the breeze hits her, the hair that lifts from her shoulders looks wispy and thin—like sheer curtains.

"Did you?" Jeremy presses.

"I—your—"

"My board. Don't tell me you forgot already. I gave it to you to paint."

My jaw flaps like a screen door with a broken hinge.

"Aura," he tsk-tsks, putting his hands on his hips, play-acting like he's a disappointed principal. "Don't tell me you're shirking your responsibilities." I look past his shoulder to find that a couple of his black-T-shirt-clad friends, who both have red baseball cap bills for faces, are fighting like hell to hold their laughter in. But Jeremy ignores them, rattling on like we're old BFFs. "It's not like you to ignore a very important assignment like that, Miss I-Skipped-A-Grade Overachiever."

"How do you know that?" I say, my forehead wrinkling so much I figure I probably look like a shar-pei.

Jeremy smiles. "I remember every little tidbit your mom dropped about you in class. I was a . . . an Aura collector. Still got everything. All the facts. All saved up. My sister puts dried-up flower petals in books, you know. To remember good days. That's what I've got, see? All these little Aura facts, like petals in a book."

Okay—what the hell do I say to something like *that*? I just stand there like some ventriloquist's doll on a shelf, my mouth hanging half-open, waiting for somebody to put their hand inside me and make some words come out.

Jeremy's friends are leaving, calling to him, and he starts to back up, even though I don't want him to. "My board," he says. "I need my *board*, all right?" before he turns and jogs right out of the Circle.

My legs are about as strong as toothpicks, but somehow, I make them turn toward Janny. Surely, I think, she heard some of that—surely she'll toss her head back and laugh that great, throaty chortle.

But Janny's still staring at her ash-coated sneakers when I walk up to her. As she has for months now, she looks covered in the dust of her now-gone happier days—just like the mermaids hanging in my kitchen at home. She's a paler, sadder version of her once glorious self. Her bloodshot eyes are as red as the pimples that dot her cheeks. And she never got rid of the forty or so extra pounds that pull at the ass of her sweatpants. Baby weight, you know. The kind of thing that makes losing your virginity to your hand seem like not such a bad thing after all.

"There's something wrong with Ethan," she says, as soon as I get within earshot, before I can blurt a syllable about Jeremy. Her voice sounds like the crack of brittle autumn twigs beneath her feet.

"How do you know?" I ask with a shrug.

"How do I *know*?" she snaps. "You know, all right, when you look at someone you're that close to. You just *know*, if you pay attention. There's something wrong with Ethan, and I should take him to a doctor, but I can't because I don't have any money right now, not even for that crappy walk-in clinic, and Mom won't listen—"

She sighs a gray cloud and tosses her cigarette into the street. She quit when she was pregnant, but afterward, in the craze of diapers and pacifiers and weird rubbery nipple things that fit on disposable bottles and Dr. Spock and baby, baby, baby, she started up again.

"I'm not dumb, you know," she informs me. "Not about this. Doesn't matter that I failed first grade. This isn't an essay exam. It's my kid."

"What about Ace?"

"Well, there's something wrong with Ace, too," she says.

"Like a virus?" I shrug.

"Sure, if assholedness catches."

The acid in her voice makes me think about the public pool, summer before last. God, I can practically smell the chlorine, almost have to blink against the sunlight that's turning the water into a giant mirror. I remember Ace Lawler in the lifeguard's seat—Ace, blond and distant. Ace, who was like a TV that could never click to life, no matter how many buttons you pushed on the remote, because he'd never been plugged into the socket in the first place.

I remember stretching out uncomfortably on my beach towel, one knee jutting up toward the sky because I couldn't stand to lie flat, my hips all spread out on the hot concrete (sometimes, voluptuous feels like *enormous*). I remember Janny dipping in the pool and pulling herself out, all arched back, hair dripping, like someone needed to take her picture right then, send it in for the next *Sports Illustrated* swimsuit issue. Her display made the lights come on behind Ace's eyes, like he was never a TV at all, but a toy monkey that just needed new batteries.

But the public pool has already been drained for the year, twice, since that fateful meeting of the soon-to-be star-crossed lovers. And now Janny looks like one of those women who's given up. One of those housewives who doesn't see the point in ever combing her hair or putting on lipstick again.

I bum a cigarette from her, just to have something to do with my stupid hands. As we stand there, it hits me how quickly everything changes—how life is like peering into a kaleidoscope, and just as you're looking at a gorgeous pattern you think you'd maybe even like to keep around forever, the colors morph into something completely different, and there's no getting back to that first pattern. No matter how much you'd like to see it again.

"Sorry," Janny finally whispers. "I'm probably miserable to be around, right now. I just—"

In the distance, the warning bell sounds. Janny grabs her backpack from the backseat of her car, tosses it over her shoulder. As we start across the field, toward Crestview, I get such a need to touch her that I grab her hand.

But Janny wrenches away, fury flashing across her eyes.

"Don't be ridiculous, Aura," she says. "We're not little kids anymore, you know."

God, do I.

4

~

An illusion is not a hallucination. In a hallucination, a schizophrenic patient sees or hears things that are real only to them. An illusion is more like seeing the world, but not being able to comprehend it. Misinterpreting everything your eyes take in, as if you were from Mars, and were trying to understand the Earth for the very first time.

I'm the first one in Wickman's Bio II class, so I flop into my chair and heave out a monster sigh. Good to be left alone for a minute, before the day officially kicks into gear. I've just barely started to relax when Angela Frieson comes clomping though Mr. Wickman's door in her blue cowboy boots with the stars all over them.

"Hey, y'all," Frieson the Freak tells me and Wickman in her Texas Hold'em accent. Instantly, I feel like a hundred jack-in-the-boxes have sprung open inside of me. I grimace as she settles into the chair next to mine, her static-laden hair standing out from her face like flower petals. I swear, she looks just like some kind of demented daisy.

I read someplace once that ugly flowers are the ones that reproduce. Everybody picks the prettiest blooms, so the uglies are the only ones that stick around in the ground long enough to spread their seed. Whole world gets uglier and uglier, all because of flower pickers. Someday, I'll look out into a meadow and see nothing but tiny little Angela Friesons. Makes me wish I could grab Frieson by her crazy blue boots and yank her right out of the ground.

But I can't because I'm stuck with her. All year—me and Frieson, lab partners extraordinaire.

This is how it happened: there are three girls in Mr. Wickman's first period Bio II. Three. Me, the Freak, and Ruby Fox. I swear that's her real name, Ruby Fox, and by God if the girl doesn't live up to it. In the ninth-grade unofficial Best of Class, she was voted Girl Most Likely to Pose for *Juggs*. And when Mr. Wickman told us to partner up back in August, the guys didn't see me or the Freak—they just saw Ruby.

So there we were, me and Frieson, in the back corner, while everybody else was pawing at Fox. Angela sighed and craned her neck, looking out at the rest of the room like surely, surely, there had to be somebody around who was better than that creepy Aura Ambrose.

Failing to find anyone better, she just moaned an "All *riiiiight*. I guess," in her crazy southern twang, and scooted her desk toward mine as we launched into our first project together—some juvenile worksheet that helped us *get to know each other.* As if Angela Frieson had time to learn anything other than what we'd be tested on—after all, the girl couldn't disrupt her 4.7 GPA.

Yeah, lucky me, I get Angela Frieson who, because of what I can only imagine was the world's most tragic scheduling conflict in the history of all time, got stuck in regular Bio II. Angela Frieson, who's auditing band so that *two* non-honors courses in the same semester (imagine the horror!) won't bring down her precious GPA. Angela Frieson, who resents that she has to have a lab partner at all, especially one that she fears she'll have to carry on her back, somebody who will get the credit for all her right answers. Angela Frieson, who is *positive* she is smarter than the entirety of the Crestview student body combined, who never once even considered the possibility that I'm no slouch in the scholastic department myself. It's just that I'm not skywriting it, or weeping about a B+ on an exam, you know?

The tardy bell lets loose its funky *blurp, blurp,* Bio II begins in full, and I'm about to scratch another notch on the top of my desk (just like the good little inmate that I am) when the Freak leans toward me and whispers (even her whisper has an accent), "Hey, Aura, I wanted to talk to you about the cat."

I guess our school gets them from the Humane Society or something. Nothing like the crawdad and the worm and the frog we dissected back in Bio I. A real cat, that somebody loved, that got in the wrong place at the wrong time. Thinking about having to dissect it—like they do in Bio II every year, no secret there—makes my skin feel prickly, like it's not just an arm or a leg that fell asleep, but my whole body.

"What about it?" I mumble.

"Listen, after we dissect it, I want it," she tells me in her awful drawl.

"What for?" I ask, my mouth all twisted up as horror breaks through me.

Angela rolls her eyes at me like she's sure my mother once dropped me on my head on a regular basis. "I'm gonna take all its skin off and put its skeleton back together."

"*Jesus*," I hiss, trying desperately not to shriek.

"Well, it's not like I'll be doin' it for *pleasure*," Angela says, the daisy petals of her hair flopping around her face. "I mean, it's the extra credit assignment. Every semester, it's the same."

"To take a poor mutilated cat home and glue it back together?" I screech.

I just stare at her, mouth open. I can't quite believe it. Take some living thing... (Okay, so the frogs and crawdads were alive at one point, too—but the cat seems different to me. I can't help it. A rat is a pig is a dog is a boy, I get that; it's a beautiful theory. But a cat's different. It just *is*.) Take some living creature and hack it up, all in the name of science. Pull its guts out to find out how they feel in your hands. Find out why they died. Find out what was good and what was off.

"*Aura*." Wickman's voice is tinged with the kind of annoyance that makes my stomach fist. My brain spins as I try to pick an expression that will convince Wickman that

I am really, truly in love with my wonderful lab partner, that I do not think she is the worst thing ever to put on a pair of blue cowboy boots, and that he should, in fact, give us both ten million extra credit points for getting along so well.

But when I look up, I realize it's not about Angela at all. Wickman's waving a green hall pass. "Your lucky day, Ms. Ambrose."

Confused, I slide out of my desk and grab the pass, which isn't just some *Please send Aura down to the main office* but a get-out-of-jail-free card. *Family Emergency*, the flowery, antique-looking script of one of the attendance secretaries proclaims.

I race through the empty hallways and burst out the front door, where the Tempo is idling.

I can smell it as soon as I open the passenger's side door—the fear. And I can hear Mom breathing—hard panting, like she's been jogging for an hour. "Get in the car," she says, through gritted teeth.

I climb in, my heart on *panic.* "What's wrong?" I ask. "Why aren't you working up a lesson for your afternoon class? What's the emergency?"

"You have to get out of there," she informs me, like she knows a masked gunman is on his way to Crestview.

"Where—school?" I stammer, even as Mom's putting the building in her rearview.

"You have to get away," she says. "Get home. But not on this street. I can fix it. But we have to go back. Scenic Avenue. Scenic. View. Back. I'll show you. I'll fix it."

I can see the wet spots on the steering wheel. Sweat from her hands as she turns off one of the main thoroughfares and winds through a quiet neighborhood with comfortable houses on huge tree-loaded lots.

When I look through the windshield, a red, plain-Jane, two-door pickup is at the opposite end of the street, heading toward us. Mom's breathing even harder, and sweat is breaking out across her face like a bad case of acne.

"Get away. Get away. Get *away*," she insists, waving her hand wildly at the driver of the pickup. "Get over!"

"It's okay, Mom," I say.

"He's in our lane!" she screams.

"He's not—" I say. "He's not even touching the line, Mom."

"He is! Oh, God!" she screams, blaring the horn. "And here we are getting smaller!" she shrieks.

"*Smaller?*"

"I'm shrinking!" she squeals.

It just doesn't make any sense. She's still Grace Ambrose, five feet nine inches tall—*legs like a supermodel,* Dad used to say. *Long, lean legs.*

"Look how small I'm getting," she shouts as the truck rolls closer.

I look down the street, at the shiny chrome grill heading straight for us, and I realize, as the hot chills light my spine on fire, that Mom's got it all backwards. She's not getting *smaller*, the truck's getting *bigger* because he's getting closer.

I want to tell her—*Mom, it's just like drawing class. Don't you remember that word you put up there on the board last weekend? "Perspective"—remember that? Close up is big, far away is small, right? He's closer now, Mom, that's all, that's all.*

"Get away!" she cries out, and veers for absolutely no reason.

My terrorized scream fills the car, along with the squealing of brakes and the crunching of a mailbox into about a billion toothpicks. The Tempo finally slides to a stop in a ditch.

Behind us, the pickup squeals, too, then turns around.

"You all right?" the driver shouts, jumping from the cab. He's the kind of guy you see in ads for politicians who swear they're down-home folks. He's wearing work boots and a ball cap with a mesh back. Has a white circle on the back pocket of his Wranglers where his daily can of Skoal goes. And from the look on his face, I'd say we scared him so bad, he just about swallowed his mouthful of chew.

"How *dare* you drive like a maniac!" Mom screams as she kicks open the Tempo's driver's side door. "How dare you come racing at me in my lane. *My lane!* How dare you shrink us!"

By this time, a woman's banging through her front screen door to get a look at her mailbox. Her mouth is open, her face all shiny with cold cream, and she's wiping her hands off on a dish towel.

"I'm sorry," I tell the owner of the pickup. "I shouldn't have let her drive." I say it with my shoulders squared, with what I hope is something that just might resemble authority.

"She ain't drunk, is she?" the guy asks. "This early in the morning?"

"No, no," I say. "You can smell her breath if you want."

"What's the matter with her?" he asks. He nods once at Mom. She's standing over the mailbox, screaming at the woman with the dish towel, "How dare you plant this thing in the middle of the road! Don't you know that's against the *law*?"

"She's having a reaction to some medication," I lie. "It wasn't this bad when we left the house—it's hitting her hard now."

"She need to get to a doctor?" the man asks.

"Sure, right. I—I really do appreciate your concern. I'm taking her right now, actually," I lie again. "Like I said, I should have been driving." Even though I've never been much of a praying kind of girl, I find myself saying a quick, silent *Please, God* that my words are all coming out strong and clear. I'm terrified—but I can act, right? Just like the troupe that fills the stone stage behind the art museum during Shakespeare in the Park on a sweet July night? If I play this thing right, I can convince the guy I'm actually Mom's *older* sister.

I guess my prayer works, because the guy nods at me like he believes I know what I'm doing. (And even if he doesn't, really, I'm taking Mom away, and he must think that, in itself, is a good thing.)

"Let me give you some money for another mailbox," I tell the woman, offering her the cash that was supposed to buy my lunch for the next two weeks.

The woman shakes her head and flicks her towel at me, like I'm being ridiculous, like we're old friends and she could never take money from me.

"Is there any way you could pull us out of this ditch?" I ask the guy with the pickup.

He doesn't say anything, just hooks the Tempo to his trailer hitch. Rev of the engine, spin of the tires, and like that, he's hauled the car out of the muddy slope.

They just stand there, the guy from the truck and the woman with the dishrag, just stand there staring as I put Mom in the passenger's seat and hurry around to the driver's side.

"Goddamn crazy men drivers," she spits, still fuming. "Men will try to own your roads, Aura. Always remember that. They will try to buy your mind. Your thoughts are roads with gravel."

And I'm barely listening, because I'm concentrating on making it seem like I'm an expert driver. I click my seat belt and reach for the gear shift, pretending I've been driving for years and years. Like this is normal, no big deal, I do it all the time.

The car lurches, even though I'm trying to press so lightly on the gas—and when I look in the rearview, there they are, the truck driver and the housewife, staring at me with their mouths scrunched up and their eyes so round, you'd think they were a couple of kids watching a horror movie.

I want to tell them, *I feel exactly the same way.*

We wiggle down the road while I'm trying to get the

knack of the steering wheel. My heart starts throwing a child's fit in my chest as a stop sign asks me to move my foot to the brake. I have no idea how hard to press the pedal or how to judge where the Tempo will finally come to rest—three blocks from the intersection? In the middle of the cross traffic? Now I'm the one leaving sweaty handprints all over the steering wheel.

I manage a halfway decent stop, and have barely begun to silently congratulate myself when Mom grabs my hand. I turn to face her, my terror exploding, because she's got this look in her eyes like she's been tied to the freaking railroad tracks.

"Don't tell your father, Aura. All right? Please, please, please, don't tell him. Promise, okay? Because I know your promises are like locks with no key. You're my girl, right? You'll help me. Okay? All right? Don't tell him, right? Promise, right, right, promise?"

"Yes, okay, yes," I finally shout. "I promise." I don't know what else to do.

5

~

Insight: A person's awareness of their illness and symptoms. When a person who has insight is told she is behaving like a stark raving lunatic, it is often enough to embarrass her into submission.

My heart is thrashing against my chest as I haul Mom up the front walk.

"Sneaky, sneaky," a man's voice lisps at me, the "*S*" sounds hissing like a pile of snakes.

When I turn, Joey Pilkington is standing on his mother's front step, shaking his finger at me. He's gotten fat these past few months. Really fat—the kind of fat where you can safely figure the guy's actually graduated to oozing bacon grease from his pores. The sight of him makes me go as tight inside as a tennis racket—and not just because the extra pounds look so bad, either.

"You steer clear of Joey," Dad warned me on a daffodil-infused spring day, when I was still wearing a little black ponytail and Joey had made his first appearance back home. "I grew up with Joey," Dad told me then. "I'm not saying he's a bad guy, but—look—steer clear, okay?"

When I was little, Joey would show up at his mom's place once, twice a year. Now the living arrangement seems permanent, even though he swears it's only until he finally turns over that new leaf.

Joey just needs time to get back on his feet, Mrs. Pilkington's always saying, like it's the chorus of her freaking life. But then again, Mrs. Pilkington is no stranger to the bottom of a bottle herself. And I guess the sobriety coins A.A. gives her when she actually makes it a month or two without drinking tend to make her a little more understanding.

Yeah, Joey Pilkington, all meth mouth and needy eyes, A.A. and N.A.'s biggest repeat failure, always just out of rehab, *poor-pitiful-me*, living out of his mother's basement. *Turn over a new leaf, my ass,* I think when I look at him. *That new leaf has been wrong-side-up so freaking long, it's grown dust.*

"You should be in school, bad girl," Joey lisps around the black remnants of broken-out front teeth. "Sneaky, sneaky," he taunts me again, like we're a couple of eight-year-olds on the playground.

I just push Mom up the steps, into the front hall. I don't know what else to do, so I steer her into the kitchen, sit her beneath the ceiling filled with wooden mermaids.

I'd rattle her shoulders to get her attention, except the way she slumps in the chair, it'd break my heart to touch her. Her whole body's so limp, she doesn't seem like she has any bones at all. She seems more like a jean jacket that's been left behind, draped over a chair.

I want to grab this jacket—no, this empty shell—and go running outside, screaming, "Wait! You forgot this!" And I want my *real* mom, the artist who teaches drawing classes and smells like the sun—to turn on her heel. "Goodness," she'd say. "How silly of me to forget this old thing." And she'd step into that empty shell I'm holding like it's a bodysuit. She'd zip up the front and smile at me. "That's better," she'd say. And life would go on as normal.

Sure. Normal. Whatever that is.

"Mom?"

She frowns. "Have you counted all those crystals yet?"

According to Mom, crystals are important, powerful objects. They have meaning and comfort and healing power—like the custard (a recipe three generations old) that Janny's mom always serves her every time she comes down with the flu. When I got strep throat, or food poisoning, or even mono from playing retarded make-out games with that douche bag Adam Riley in the ninth grade, Mom gave me crystals to hold. But somehow, already, I know she's not talking about those kinds of crystals. Not the sharp, jagged quartz pieces that Mom swears she can feel vibrate.

"What crystals, Mom?"

"Crystals of *sugar*," she says, shocked that I'm suddenly so stupid. She reaches across the table, picks the lid up off the old ceramic bowl, and points at the white mound inside. "Haven't you counted them yet?"

"Every single little crystal?" I ask, fighting the hot chills.

"You won't know how much to buy if you don't count them, the crystals," she snaps.

I'm looking right at her, but Mom seems so far away. It's like she's still on that vacation to Florida. But the thing is, she doesn't ever have to come back. She can just step off the eastern Florida coast and dip her toes into a corner of the Bermuda Triangle, never to be heard from again.

Staring at her, I miss her so much, I ache. If I could, I'd write her a postcard: *Dear Mom, having a rotten time without you. Wish you were here.*

"Sure, I counted," I tell her, smearing a fake grin across my cheeks, à la kid in a Welch's grape juice ad. "Seven thousand fourteen."

Mom looks at me, a little shocked. But she finally nods her head, once, like she thinks she's really taught me a lesson.

"You know what you are?" I ask her. "Exhausted. Teaching three afternoons a week at the museum, *and* all weekend long—*plus* keeping up with your own artwork... I think you should call in those—" I stop myself from saying *sick days.* "Vacation. You must have a few days coming to you, right?"

Mom offers a limp nod.

Actually, it's wrong to leave the museum in the lurch, scrambling to get someone to fill in. But even if they got mad enough to do something really horrible—like maybe dock her pay—we'd at least still have Dad's child support to lean on.

"What can work more magic than some time off? *Vacation*... by Saturday, you'll feel as bright as a rhinestone. Actually, *I'll* call the museum," I offer. "One less thing for you to deal with. Nobody can recognize the difference between your voice and mine, anyway.

"Why don't you just go lie down?" I suggest. "When you get up, I'll have lunch waiting for you." It's not like I'm going to get back to school today, anyway.

She pulls her empty shell of a body up, and leaves the kitchen. But instead of taking a nap, Mom slams the door of her room and launches this Janis Joplin rocket—that's what it sounds like, anyway. "Me and Bobby McGee" streaks through the house, whistling until it hits the kitchen, where it explodes. I feel like I ought to duck and cover somewhere, because, I swear, Janis sings like a regular guided missile streaking across the sky.

As the chorus of the song flowers, I feel like I'm at a concert for the dead and Janis is right there in front of me, wearing a feather headdress and big round pink sunglasses, a bottle of Southern Comfort tucked under her arm.

I can see those words Mom wrote on the board last

weekend: *PERSPECTIVE, PEPPER, PET.* And my hand is suddenly reaching for the phone, and I'm halfway through my dad's number—the one that rings in the insurance office across town—before I stop, wondering what the hell I think the guy's going to do, since he's so far away now.

And he *is* far, you know—has been ever since my last soccer game. The last time I'd ever been part of a team that had won anything, victoriously pulling ourselves away from a tie. Not that Dad had been there to see it. He was working, still painting houses—unhappily, though, by that point. He'd already sold all his philosophy books at our last garage sale, calling them *pie in the sky.* He'd bought a briefcase, and had started writing a résumé. He'd bought a sport jacket, of all things.

But Mom was in the stands. I raced to her, like my teammates were racing to their own mothers, even though we were in middle school by then. Even though we were finding we didn't need Kleenex to fill our bras so much anymore; even though we were definitely getting the hang of eye shadow and curling irons; even though we'd all had at least one crush, and a select few of us even had someone to call *boyfriend.* We weren't our mamas' little girls anymore. But my team was so big-bright-yellow-sunflower happy, no one even thought about shrugging her mother's hug away.

And I was no different, me, twelve years old, racing up the bleachers. "Mom," I said, my heart so joyful it bounced, just like a soccer ball off a knee. "Let's go." I pointed out all the other mothers and daughters who were stepping off the field. Cars were starting, cranking to life, one after another. Minivans and SUVs were leaving. Off for pizza, off for ice cream, off to celebrate the good news—*we won, we won.* God, the pattern of the words—*we won, we won*—it sounded like feet that skipped, you know? Like the very sound that bliss itself would make.

"I can't, Aura," Mom whispered. "I'll drown. I'll drown in that shiny water." And she pointed at the rows of bleachers below her.

Waves of nausea began to swell in my gut, causing my legs to wobble. *Please, Mom, does it have to be today? Do we really have to go through this now, when everything is so good and so pure and we won—don't you know we won? Did you see any of it? Did you believe it? Or did you just think you imagined it all?*

"Come on, Mom," I tried again. "Come on, let's go."

"*No,*" Mom insisted. "No. Not ever. I'll drown in that shiny water."

When I turned, to show her she could leave, that it wasn't water at all, but bleachers that would hold her, Mom grabbed hold of my wrist. "Don't, Aura, please. Don't go out there. There are alligators in that shiny water!"

"Okay, Mom," I whispered, goose bumps making a polka-dot pattern all over my sweaty skin. I sat next to her and pulled our cell phone out of her purse. "I'll call Dad," I told her.

"*Yes,*" she whispered. "He'll help. Tell him to rent a boat."

"We're still at the soccer field," I told Dad when he

answered the cell he kept clipped to the pocket of his coveralls. "And we can't leave, because of the—the shiny water."

But Dad didn't say, all worried, like I still expected him to, "I'll be right there." He just sighed, long and exasperated, right in my ear. Sighed so hard I could practically feel his breath, hot, coming through the phone. "Aura, I can't."

"You—you—" I stuttered.

"I'm not even working in town today, Aura. I'm all the way over in Billings. And I can't just keep running off at a moment's... Look, you're going to have to handle it, okay?"

My whole body was thudding and I was so scared, so scared, suddenly *I* was the one who was drowning. *I can't, I can't. You're not really going to do this, are you? Why are you going to let everything fall on my shoulders, heavy as every brick building in the whole world?*

"You're going to have to talk her down, okay?"

"She won't—"

"She will, Aura. She just needs you to show her what's real. Tell her that I said to trust you. Tell her that this is an episode. She knows what that means, okay?"

"*No,*" I begged. "Don't leave us out here. *Please.*"

And my dad—the selfish, unfeeling jerk—*hung up on me.*

The whole world was wrong in that moment. Everything was off—the smell of grass was so strong in my nose, it was like fumes from nail polish remover.

"Is he coming?" Mom asked. "Is he bringing the boat?"

And I started to cry, because everyone else in the world was gone by then, and there was no one I could even call out to—not a coach and not another mother. Nobody, just me and Mom, but she was seeing a whole other world, one that I wasn't a part of, which made me feel like she wasn't inches but a whole universe away. At that moment, I felt so abandoned—like Pluto must have when all the scientists decided it wasn't a planet anymore. Nothing but a bunch of cosmic trash.

We sat for what felt like months, until darkness fell—but not because the sun was setting. No, like some cosmic joke, the sky that had been so perfectly blue for our game was filled with black, churning clouds. And the strong, overwhelming smell of grass was overpowered by the smell of wet clouds, approaching rain.

We were both bawling when the rain started to fall. Crying like a couple of babies, the downpour soaking us to our very bones. And I prayed, like an idiot or a poor pitiful soul with no choices left. I prayed that at any minute, Dad would come streaking down the street, driving the company truck so erratically that the ladder would fall from the top, clatter straight to the pavement as he veered toward the soccer field. There he'd be, big work boots clomping up the bleachers, and even in the dark, I'd be able to see the worry-wrinkles all over his face.

But he didn't. There was no point in wishing anymore. Time to find some sort of exit strategy.

What was that word he'd used?

"An ... an ep ... an episode," I mumbled.

Mom turned to me, her eyes wide, like she'd just torn up the winning lottery ticket—two hundred million dollars in tiny little pieces at the bottom of the waste can.

I've got her.

"That's not water," I said, my words attacking her like boxing punches that she could never dodge. If this was a battle of the wills, *I* was going to win.

"You can walk on it, really," I told her, standing up and squirming away when she tried to grab me. "Look at me. I'm fine. I'm not drowning. It looks like water, but it's really just the bleachers. Remember our soccer game? You came up here to watch our game. And we won, Mom," I said, trying to smile, even though the rain felt like nails against my skin and I was still crying a little. "We won. Let's go home, okay? Let's go home."

Remembering how I'd wrapped my arms around her that day—*me*—just like all the mothers had wrapped their arms around their daughters and led them away from the soccer field, I put the phone back on the cradle. What was I thinking? Why would I even consider the possibility of getting help from Dad? I'd just as easily get help from a pair of salad tongs.

In Mom's room, I grab the phono needle and pull the arm to the side to cut the music, but not far enough to click the turntable off. The label of *Pearl* just keeps spinning.

The record player's a real antique—Mom clutches onto it like a kid with a security blanket. And she's truly got an amazing assortment of vinyl, for anyone into collecting—Hendrix and Pink Floyd and The Velvet Underground.

Rare gems like a promotional issue of the Stones' *Sticky Fingers* album with the zipper on the front, and a signed copy of Dylan's *Bringing It All Back Home*. She's even got an old Beatles butcher cover. I could probably go to college out of state on what's in that stack. But Mom would never part with it. And who am I to ask Mom to part with anything else? I mean, how many of us have to wave goodbye to our hold on reality?

"Too loud," Mom says, and tosses her angry face at me with such force, it feels like I've just been smacked with a wayward soccer ball.

"No, it's not," I insist. "I turned it off—see, Mom? No more music."

She cringes like feedback from mile-high Marshall amps is screeching right into her brain. I wish I could help her, turn the volume down on the thoughts that come to her like a radio cranked up far too loud.

But then she shakes her head, like a dog trying to knock water out of her ears, grabs a box of art supplies, and starts furiously dumping tubes of oils and acrylics on the floor and opening paint cans. She dunks a brush into a small container of a dark metal-gray. When she pulls it back out, she lets it drip all over some bunched-up mounds of drop cloth like she's making her own Jackson Pollock.

"I know how to fix it. Everything. Fine," she says. And her eyes—if I ever came across a wild animal with eyes like hers, I'd back away slowly, heart pounding in every one of my fingers and toes.

"Mom," I tell her, "you're having an episode, okay? Like

in the car this morning? What you saw when we ran off the road? Why you pulled me out of class? This whole thing is an episode."

"Leave me alone," she snaps, and drops the needle on the vinyl. She grabs the volume knob and cranks it up so loud, she'll never be able to hear me, no matter how loud I screech.

6

~

One of the main risk factors for developing schizophrenia is having a close relative completely messed up by the disease.

The front door explodes with a furious knock. When I swing it open, I find our next-door neighbor, Mrs. Pilkington, standing on our porch in her purple velour jogging suit, her poofy gray bangs hanging floppy and crooked over her forehead. "Whash going on in there?" she slurs, pointing to the lab puppy at her feet. "You're hurting Scooter's earsh."

Is she serious?

"I... I'm gonna call a copsh," she swears through her whiskey-drenched stupor. Her face looks like a sculpture made out of Crisco that's been set outside during the hottest part of a hundred-degree summer day.

"Don't do that," I say. "I'll turn it down—I'm sorry."

Sure, she's a lousy drunk. And maybe, if she were to complain, the cops would only roll their eyes at her. But then again, maybe the cops really would come inside my house, and they'd see what state Mom's in—before I could figure out how to fix it—and they'd wind up hauling her off. Slapping a straitjacket on her. Trying to fry her brain back into working order with some good old-fashioned electroshock.

And if Mom were locked up, what would happen to me? Not to sound like the mayor of Snootsville, but I really don't know what would be worse—foster care, or life with Dad (the vanilla ice cream cone) and Brandi (a bubble blown from an obnoxious pink wad of chewing gum).

I burst into Mom's room and yank the power cord on the record player.

"Gimme that," I say, reaching for the brush. "Come on, you've got the Pilkingtons all worked up. You've got to quit."

"No," she snaps. "Don't you dare take this from me." But the words run much deeper than a brush. She's not talking about a wooden handle and some bristles. These words have come straight up from the darkest part of her, the core of her very being, and they bubble up to the surface wearing soul moss. She's talking about her *art*. "I need this," she whispers.

I let go, watch her grab a tube of paint and squirt a

thick stream of yellow straight onto the bristles. But it seems like she's forgotten about Janis, at least, so I leave her.

The morning weighs so heavily on me that I feel like Atlas, holding the entire freaking sky up on my shoulders. My canvas bag is on the table with my bio textbook poking out the top. I reach inside, pull out my sketchbook, and collapse into it, the way I've seen Ethan sometimes collapse into Janny's chest. Art, the great soother, comforter. Art, the thing that makes me whole—just like Mom.

Lately, when I pick up a pencil, artwork and poetry have shown up like vines, twisting in between each other so tightly that if I were going to try to uproot one, yank it off the page, the other would go, too. I start sketching—a rocking horse—back and forth, sane and insane, here and gone. And underneath, a poem explodes across the page, frantic and angry:

I can see the shadows again,
Masked dancer swaying in the breeze.

Imagination running wild,
Defying gravity.
Mirages in her eyes,
Hand-in-hand with reality.

As always, breathing is a little easier as my pencil flies. The ache of my life quits pulsing. As I draw, and as words come with my images, it's as though I've been given a cortisone shot—the pain is gone. I can move. I don't feel completely crippled anymore.

But then I lift my head, and through the sliding glass back door I can see Mrs. Pilkington in her own backyard with Scooter, staggering, pointing at the tree, like that's all the instruction the guy needs to be housebroken. Joey comes outside, back screen flopping, voice like an angry father's, and he's shouting at her, something about *meeting, meeting, sponsor.* They seesaw this way, taking turns—first Joey's off the wagon, then his mom, the sober one screaming in the driveway when the drunk one finally rolls in at five a.m. with vomit trailing down the front of their shirt.

They're just alike. I'm shivering, all hot chills as I hurry away from my sketch and walk back down the hall to my own bedroom. But mine's a bizarre room, really—not any real sanctuary at all—with kelly green carpet and a pale blue ceiling and flowers Mom pulled me out of bed to paint when I was in the third grade, after that lightning bolt of inspiration had struck her. Flowers with wild polka-dotted petals, stamens making giant curlicues. Lady bugs as big as monkeys. Clouds swirling like wisps of blue cotton candy.

We'd painted all night, while Dad was visiting an old friend in Albuquerque. Or Mom did, really. I watched and carried paint trays and added white or red or orange when she told me to, mixing the new hues for her with the end of a ruler. Proud, back then, to just be part, you know?

"Can't take it," Mom's muttering angrily from her room just across the hall. "Can't. From me. Mine. Don't. I'll fix it. Everything. Fine." I remember the way Joey screamed his sloshy, drunken words at his mother the summer before last, dawn spilling like orange Kool-Aid across the sky. "You can't *make* me quit," he'd said, just like some little boy. "You can't *make* me." Even though the booze and the who-knows-what-else he was on was obviously going to kill him. Even though addiction has always been the damn cause of every one of the Pilkingtons' problems.

I wander back across the hall to reassure her—or maybe it's to reassure me—that we're okay. I come up from behind her, and start to wrap my hands around her long black hair, putting it into a kind of temporary ponytail, just like she used to do to me when I was little.

She pushes me away, her eyes so crazed, *crazed*, that my first instinct is to snatch that brush away from her again. But I remember the sketchbook on the kitchen table, and I know all too well how she would feel if I were to take it, to trash her art supplies. It'd be like gouging her eyes out.

So I turn, and leave her with her painting. Which I'm slowly beginning to realize is like shutting the door while she sticks a hypo needle filled with poison into her arm.

7

~

Famous schizos: van Gogh, painter. Jack Kerouac, author. Syd Barrett, musician of Pink Floyd fame. Vaclav Nijinsky, dancer. Every single freaking one of them an artist of some sort.

"Aura," Janny sighs. "It's not like I can just take off—to—what? Hang out?" In the background, Ethan is screaming like somebody's put a knife through his skull.

"Your mom'll babysit," I say, selfishly. "I just—I need somebody else to look at her, you know? Just come over for dinner—real quick—and you can take off."

"*Now,* Aura? You're handing me this now."

I get tight inside, defensive. It's not like I planned this. It's not like I *want* to have a mother who's in her room, starting canvases and leaving them half-finished, paint flying everywhere. It's not like I want a mom who wakes me up like she did last night, rustling me out of bed, hissing, "Aura—Aura—I need some green. Are you listening? You need to get in the car, okay?"

What I wanted to say was, *Yeah, Mom, this town is full of all-night art supply stores. Because everybody knows that at two a.m., you just might find yourself needing a bottle of cough syrup, some ibuprofen, a jug of milk, or a tube of acrylic kelly green #304. Right.* But I just peeled myself from my sheets and tried to placate her by mixing up some green myself. *Yellow and blue, Mom. Don't you remember?*

"Ten minutes," I tell Janny. "Five," I try to bargain. "You can just pretend to eat." I feel like some wayward stray at her back door, scratching and pawing and begging. And that makes me angry, too. Hadn't I let Janny cry into my shoulder for a week solid when the stick had turned pink?

"Fine," Janny sighs, exasperated, just the same way she sighs at her mother. I figure, judging by her tone, I even get an eye roll.

I mix up a tuna noodle casserole, and while it melts into a bubbling, canned-fish blob, I head into the living room and sit down on the bench of the Ambrose Original, our family piano. I really don't play the old upright very well. I can read the treble clef okay and can form a few chords. But the real reason I love it—as pitiful as it is—is because I built it with Dad. Because he bought it for my tenth birthday. Because I came home from school, and there it was, all scraggly and chewed up, looking like it had been through every major battle of World War II. And for more than a year, we spent every Saturday going to Piano Pete's—an old music store just across the street from the skankiest used car dealership in town—to buy pedals, hammers, felts, damper pads, strings.

When I sit on the bench, I remember how Dad and I used to laugh about the belt buckle Pete wore, the gold thing in the shape of a baby grand. I remember how Mom sanded the mahogany down to the nubs so that she could paint it up in her own amazing style. She did, too—angels and sinners and street performers and love and pain and fear and lust and everything everybody ever played a song about—she painted it all, an absolute masterpiece, right there on the piano. I think about how we got it done in time to play carols on it. All Christmas Eve long.

I stare at the *Ambrose Original* lettering Mom free-handed over the *Kimball* that was branded to the front when Dad first brought it home. I touch the perfect, straight, strong, gold brushstrokes while my eyes wander over the rest of Mom's painting. The way the colors swirl across the top of the piano, it's always reminded me a little of the van Gogh that shows up in all the print stores—*Starry Night.*

Yeah, van Gogh, schizo as they ever come. Some say that's why he cut off his ear, you know—because he was tired of the voices. And they—the ever-present *THEY*—so-called experts who probably can't even tie their own shoes—they say that *Starry Night* shows how light's texture can change with the onset of a psychotic episode.

Damn, I hate that picture.

I wonder sometimes why some people are geniuses, and

some are just nuts. What's so different about Mom and van Gogh? What's in the sunflower paintings that didn't make it to any one of the hundreds of canvases Mom's stacked everywhere—the garage and the living room and the attic? Why isn't my room considered a masterpiece? Why aren't vacationers from Pittsburgh and Little Rock lining up at our door in their Bermuda shorts, salivating over a chance to get a glimpse of the garden Mom painted all over my bedroom walls? Why am I not standing at the door every single weekend, taking money and telling everyone, *Remember, no flash photography, thank you*?

The clunkerty-clunk of the engine in Janny's rattle-bang p.o.s. makes me remember dinner. She throws open the front door just as I rush back into the kitchen to pull the casserole from the oven.

"Where is she?" Janny sighs, rubbing at her face. She looks like she's forty, the way that pretty face of hers has been stretched and bloated with the pain of a mistake that never gets undone.

"She's been painting ever since we got home yesterday—her eyes," I start to babble, explaining about the car ride and how I had to drive.

"That's really dumb," Janny says, pulling a pack of cigarettes from her floppy, bargain-bin purse—the kind of thing we would have made fun of a couple of years ago, made from scraps of mismatched leather sloppily patched together. She shoves aside the back screen so that she can smoke through the open door. "You don't know the first thing about driving," she grumbles, because she's already had her license for a year and a half. Pre-Ethan, the twenty months in our age difference (caused by Janny getting held back once and me skipping a grade) never seemed like it even existed, since, from the time we met, we were always in the same class. Now, though, she's holding those twenty crappy months over my head. Like somehow she's already seen it all, and I'm just this snot-nosed little kid.

"What was I supposed to do?" I snap while Janny flicks her half-smoked cigarette onto the patio. "Out there in the middle of some ditch."

Janny flashes me a principal face, like I should know better. I feel a little like slapping her for it, actually.

While Janny sets the table, I head down the hall, saying, "Mom? Mom?" my voice as soft as the fur on a tottery young kitten.

"Mom," I say again as I slip into her doorway.

But she doesn't answer. I just stare at her awhile, covering my mouth, because after a full day of painting she seems as wasted as Joey Pilkington after a night out. My eyes travel across the paint she's smeared up her arms and under her fingernails and all over her face. She's tied her hair in a knot, too—an honest-to-God knot, and it's been so long since she's put any conditioner on her hair, I figure she'll probably have to whack it all off. I figure her hair, dry as yarn, won't ever come out of what she's done to it.

I guess that's the beauty of a knot, really. It never comes undone.

Mom's taken her jeans off and is wearing some crazy-looking housedress, fourteen times too big. I wonder where it's come from—it looks old, like she could have found it in the attic, but also stained with grease, like Dad used it as a rag when he was still around to work on the car. And it hits me that it looks like a maternity dress. Like she wore it when she was nine months pregnant with me. I get the hot chills all over again, because as she glances up, I'm not sure who she thinks I am. I wonder if she's somehow lost in time. I wonder if she even remembers that I was born, that I'm hers.

Then again, I try to tell myself, *maybe she grabbed the old dress because it looked like a comfortable thing to paint in.*

As we stare at each other, I find myself wishing that Mom could somehow *pretend* to be sane. It's a wasted wish, like squeezing your eyes shut and hoping that when you open them again, *poof!* You'll have traveled back in time.

Still, though, the whole world is full of posers. People who lie on Internet dating sites. People who fudge their real weight on their driver's licenses. People who drive rented sports cars to their high school reunions, acting like they're more successful than they really are. So maybe, just maybe, me and Mom could pretend to be normal.

My eyes settle on the pockets on her housedress. Big pockets, open at the top. And because I can feel desperation knocking on the door of my heart, I quietly slide one of her drawers open and pull out a crystal from her collection—one of those rocks she swears she can feel vibrate, she swears has power, can heal. I slip it into one of her enormous pockets.

I mean, even if I'm not exactly sure I believe in this

stuff, *she* does. And that's what makes all the difference, isn't it? Her belief? Isn't it what's governing my whole damn life—the shadows Mom believes in?

I finally manage to steer her out of her room, down the hall, and into a kitchen chair. An October evening breeze comes through the screen door, rattling the driftwood mermaids above the table. I pull the sliding glass shut, dole out heaps of steaming casserole.

"We can't sit long," Mom insists. "The world will stop."

Janny's fork pauses midair.

"Our feet. Everyone's feet," Mom says. "We all take steps, only we're not just pushing *ourselves* forward. We're pushing the world, see? We're pushing the whole world forward. If men and women and animals die from the world completely, the earth will stop moving. It takes *us* to move the world, to propel it forward. Like how you pedal a bicycle, see? We've got to pedal the earth!"

"Mom," I say. "Let's eat dinner, okay?"

Mom leans forward, her eyes wild. "What about her?" she whispers, pointing at Janny. "Do you see *her*? Because I do, I can, but I might paint her later if she's okay to be real for a little while."

"Mom," I say quietly. "That's Janny. You know Janny."

I can hear Janny gulp even from across the table—what's harder to swallow, I wonder, my mom or my tuna?

Janny sucks in a deep breath and pushes her scraggly brown hair behind her ears, and she does try. God love her, in that moment, she smiles and says, "Could you please pass the salt? Grace? Pass the salt, please."

Mom stands up, her face lighting up like she's just had the biggest epiphany of her entire life. "You know, if I tried hard enough, I think I could change the course of the whole world. *Think*," she says, stepping out into the middle of the linoleum. "If I just spin hard enough, fast enough, in the opposite direction—"

She starts twirling in her bare feet, squealing like she's the fastest thing on the whole planet—faster than bullets or pain or fear.

Janny makes this terrible face as she fights her tears. God, she fights as hard as some people battle cancer. But the tears break through, anyway.

"I just want the salt," Janny cries out. "*Salt!*" She screams it with such power, I think for sure she's ripped her vocal cords right in two. She jumps up and throws her napkin on the table, still screaming—not words, just screaming, like a woman in a haunted house.

I grab the shaker where it's still sitting beside Mom's plate. But Janny's already snatched her purse up and she's heading for the door.

Wait wait wait wait wait.

Janny races down the front steps and I follow, like a dope, the salt shaker still in my hand. *Here, Janny, here's your salt, take it, I want you to have it always and forever.*

"I *can't* anymore," Janny says. "I can't be around her, all right?"

"Why? What's the deal? You used to stand up for me, you know."

"God, Aura, because—because it's too *hard* for me, okay? I can't deal with her anymore. Not now, not with everything else."

"What else?" I scream. "Really! What? Your kid's got what—a stuffy nose, Janny? But my mom—*help* me!"

"You don't know what you're talking about," she yells, tears dripping off her chin. "You don't know everything."

"I know you're a shitty-ass friend."

Janny wipes her face and nods. "Then I guess you won't miss me much, will you?" she asks. She raises her arms a little, just to let them fall to her sides—*such a final sound.*

"I'm goin' to Ace's," she says.

I stand there on the step, hoping like hell I look defiant and solid as Janny climbs into her p.o.s. When her car rattle-bangs around the corner, disappearing into the night, I scream and slam the stupid shaker on the front walk. Under the moon, the salt glistens even brighter than the broken shards of glass.

I collapse into a pile of blubbery tears on the step, just as the front door opens behind me. Mom wraps her paint-drenched arms around my neck. "It's okay—I know how things break, mine break, we're so alike, you promised, remember? You promised, right?"

8

~

Scientists have discovered that the same flexibility in thought that leads to creativity can also lead, in some individuals, to mental illness.

My chest is heaving as I leaf through the pages I printed out last night. All my Googling has resulted in one clear line, and it runs straight through schizos and artists both. *Mad genius,* my pages shout. *Schizophrenia and the artistic temperament. Creativity and psychopathology.* I feel like throwing up.

I'd started my search to help her. I mean, for Christ's sake, there's an herb for everything, right? Echinacea for colds. Bilberry for eyesight. Ginger for a metabolism boost. So I figured I could get her something. Pick it up in the vitamin aisle of Walmart. But then I started running into this other stuff—and all of a sudden, I'm wondering about me.

Because the thing is, genetics are only part of it. One risk factor. I've always known—white-coats had always assured Dad and me—that environmental forces play their role, too. And now I'm starting to wonder, *what* kind of environmental forces? Drawing? Writing? Sketching? Hammering chords on the Ambrose Original? It suddenly seems like my whole life I've been a smoker, only nobody's bothered to tell me what smoking does to the lungs. I've spent the past fifteen years begging for disease to flower inside of me.

And the worst part in this whole stinking mess is that I can't even talk to Janny about it. I tried to call her, sure, because it isn't like we've never had a fight before. But when her mom answered the phone, I could hear Janny scream, "I'm *not* talking to that selfish bitch. Hang up the phone. Hang it *up*."

"Aura, sweetie," Mrs. Jamison tried, syrupy as a short stack, like I was eight.

"Forget it," I'd sighed, trying to convince myself Janny just needed time to cool. But when I'd walked up on the Circle this morning, she'd flicked her cigarette and run off before I had time to catch up.

"Hey, Aura," Frieson the Freak hisses.

I jump, realize that Wickman's got Bio II in full swing (when did the tardy bell even ring?), and start shoving the pages from my Internet search into my canvas bag.

"*Aura,*" Frieson hisses again.

"*What?*" I hiss back.

"We okay about the cat?"

The way Angela's so obsessed with dissections makes me feel like *my* skin is getting peeled off. Because I know all those white-coats Mom's seen over the years would love to hack into her, pull her brain right out of her head and hold it to the light, point to some circuit and say *Here, right here. This is where it all went wrong.*

And after what I read last night, I know they'd like to get their hands on me, too. They—no, not they—Angela. As I sit there staring at Angela, I can see us, twenty years down the road, me on the carving table and her a real M.D., or maybe one of those autopsy CSI guys. Only her coat wouldn't really be a doctor's coat at all—it would be more like a butcher's coat, covered in red splatter.

"I asked to get you," Angela would tell me. "All the way back in junior year, I asked Mr. Wickman if I could get you to dissect—I got dibs, way back then. You're mine, now that you've gone crazy, too, just like your mama, just like you were destined to be."

Too anxious to even bother to roll up her sleeves, she would jab me with her knife and make that giant "Y" incision down my chest.

"Aura?" Angela persists. "We agree, right? When the time comes, I'm gonna get the cat?"

"Take it, already," I spit. "Don't let me stand in the way of your sick dream."

"*Aura Ambrose.*" When I look up, Wickman's holding

another green pass. All I can think of is that awful car ride with Mom.

"At some point, I'll get you in here for a full class," Wickman says beneath his brown moustache, a relic from the days when *Magnum, P.I.* ruled the tube. I'm frozen, until he rattles the pass. "Come on. Hurry up. Mrs. Fritz wants to talk to you."

Great. My counselor, Queen of the Anti-Gypsies, wants to talk. This can't be good—it can't. My whole stomach turns into the board game of Chutes and Ladders—all ups and downs, topsy-turvy. I'm about to get reamed...

I scoop up my notebooks and slide out of the room. One good thing about being sent to my fate is that at least I won't have to imagine the Freak dressed up like a character out of *Macbeth*, stirring a boiling cauldron of dead cats.

Down the stairs, around the corner to the main office. *Mrs. Fritz,* the sign over the first door on the right announces. *Counselor, A–C.* Yeah, Fritz, as in: broken, not in working order. *This cheap-ass TV is always on the fritz.*

Mrs. Fritz's office is full of red and white pom-poms and those cheerleading skirts with all the pleats. She's got signs up all over her walls—*Second Place, All-State Championship. First Place, Citywide Cheer-Fest.* Because she's their sponsor, you know, the cheerleaders. Which is pretty funny, considering that Mrs. Fritz is the kind of fat old gal that makes you stare at her pantyhose-covered legs while she drones on in her nasal voice. You just stare and stare, thinking that anytime now, those brown legs are going to pop—I mean, pantyhose can only stretch so far. And then surely they'd pop, right? Just like a balloon with too much air? One more sip of the gigantic Dr Pepper she keeps on her cluttered desktop and *WHOP!* Mr. Groce, the security guard, would come racing in, 9-1-1 already dialed on his cell phone, because he was sure we were all in the midst of another Columbine.

Oh, never mind, he'd tell the operator when he looked inside Fritz's office. *Janet just blew her hose, is all.*

"Aura Ambrose," I say, holding the slip.

"Come on in, dear," Fritz says, making me wish to God that the faculty members could find another pet name. I mean, what is it with that word, anyway? I've never called anybody *dear* in my life. Is it a sign of age, I wonder, like crow's feet and varicose veins? Do you just open your mouth one day and out it comes, like vomit, even though you're trying to hold it back, but there it is, all sloppy and nasty, this sign that suddenly you're an old woman?

She points to a seat next to the door. As I sit down, I check the clock. Two minutes have passed already since I got her note. Two whole minutes I haven't been thinking about Janny, or Angela's dissections, or even Mom, and in that moment, I'm actually grateful to Mrs. Fritz, because she has such fat legs and she uses the word *dear* and it takes my mind away from everything in my life that sucks.

"I was contacted by Mrs. Kolaite a few days ago," she starts as she unwraps a bacon, egg, and cheese Burger King Croissan'Wich.

Ah, here we go, here we go. Mrs. Kolaite (rhymes with *ol' lady*) is just the kind of uptight stickler who would've blabbed to my counselor that I've got five post-lunch tardies to her English class. Every single stupid time I'm late to one of Kolaite's thrilling lessons on onomatopoeia, she purses her lips and tosses a disgusted look at me, her stub of a chin sinking so deep into her fleshy throat that it disappears completely. But it's not like I'm wrapped up in some vapid teenage cafeteria crap—*hairdos* and *can I borrow your silk cami on Friday* and *guess who isn't a virgin anymore.* No, I have a best friend who rants about her son all through lunch and snaps at me, "What, my problems don't interest you?" when I try to leave because the clock says it's time for me to get my hiney back to class.

Correction: I *had* a best friend. Wait—is that really what happened last night?

"Yeah," I tell Fritz, "the tardies. I know. Kolaite told me she might make me do an extra assignment—an essay on *Billy Budd* or something." *And I'll take it in a second, if it means I can get out of your office. I'll smile and tell you some whopper like "I find that literary critique is just like dietary fiber—I just can't get enough of it into my life."*

"Mrs. Kolaite actually didn't mention the tardies," Fritz frowns. "But punctuality is an incredibly important part—"

"So—" I interrupt. "If that's not it—"

"Yes," Fritz says. "The *real* reason I called you to my office." She pauses for effect and to take another slurp of her Dr Pepper. "Mrs. Kolaite contacted me about your papers, your work. You're a very creative young lady, Ms. Ambrose."

My mouth turns into a desert. "I don't understand." I watch as Fritz takes an enormous bite of her croissant. I guess if I'd been assigned to any of the other counselors, I'd be offended. I mean, it is pretty rude for a faculty member to be eating in front of the kid she just hauled out of class. It's not like I have all morning to watch her chow down. But with Fritz, food is like a pair of shoes, or lipstick, because it's her constant accessory. No one in the history of Crestview has ever known her breath to smell like toothpaste instead of onions, or for her fingernails to be painted with red polish instead of marinara sauce.

"Mrs. Kolaite showed me a short story you wrote for class," she says when she finally swallows.

I go cold in my feet. "I had to write it, it was an assignment—"

"And your notes. Mrs. Kolaite is in the habit of collecting your class notes, isn't she?"

"Yes, but—"

"You take very good notes—astute notes, in your own words. And you still have time, each class period, to write free verse poetry and create beautiful sketches in the margins."

"Doodles, that's all—my mind wanders away from me—I know I shouldn't—"

"Oh, there's nothing about this that looks like a doodle, Aura," she says, showing me a sketch I did quickly of Mrs. Kolaite's face—a profile I'd done without thinking or even meaning to, down the margin of a pop quiz. "I took it upon myself to show this little masterpiece to our art instructors, and they both want to know why you haven't enrolled in a single drawing or painting course at Crestview."

Okay, my whole face is going to ignite at any minute. Explode and send tiny little fireballs dancing through Fritz's office.

"Dad wanted me to take real courses," I say, which is true. The dad of old—the one who painted houses and quoted the great philosophers and marveled at what Mom could do with a canvas—the dad I'd maybe even loved—he *wanted* me to be creative. But the new dad, who sells insurance and drives through town in his ridiculously overpriced hybrid SUV, he'd frowned in absolute disapproval at the Art I that I'd put on my schedule last spring.

"Get real, Aura," he spat. "Just—take something practical, why don't you? How about Keyboarding?" He clicked his pen and marked over my schedule before I could argue. *Did he know something? About what art could do to me? Why didn't he tell me?*

"Art *is* a real class," Fritz protests. "And you have such obvious natural ability that it seems a shame—"

"I don't have any natural ability at all," I tell Fritz sharply.

"Ms. Ambrose, Mrs. Kolaite thinks you ought to be in our accelerated arts and letters program. She thinks you should be in honors English, and our art instructors all agree—"

"Look, I don't want to be in that, okay?" I snap.

Fritz looks shocked, like I've just asked her how she

gets her fat ass in those pantyhose every morning, anyway. *I mean, really—are they sprayed on permanently?*

"In my experience, students who have artistic ability also usually *like* to take part in art courses or writing courses," Fritz protests. "And in the long run, it would help. Why, art schools and liberal arts universities really do like to see that a student has a background in these kinds of subjects. It could give you a real leg up when you start to apply to college." While she's talking, she's rummaging around on her desk, balling up McDonald's sandwich wrappers and throwing them in her wastebasket, picking up stacks of paper and tossing them aside.

"And it seems to me," she says, pausing to take yet another sip of her Dr Pepper, "it seems that I remember another Ambrose—maybe at the art museum? Is there some talent that runs in the family?"

There's something absolutely menacing about the way she's smiling at me, something horrific, like she's got me in her clutches. Like she knows every single last awful detail about my crummy life. *Is that what this whole thing is about? The apple doesn't fall far from the tree?*

"Yeah, well, I don't have any inherited ability, all right?" I snap. "And I *don't* like it. Drawing, writing, whatever. I hate it. I don't want any part of it. Thank you for your time." These last few words should sound polite, but I say them with such hatred it's like I'm telling her *Fuck off, you fat cow.* Cradling my notebooks, I stomp out of her office and down the hallway.

I'm so pissed off, I can't stomach the thought of going

back upstairs and sitting next to Angela Frieson while she licks her chops and sharpens her dissecting knife in her mind. So I veer straight toward the back exit and push the bar on the door, which trips the alarm. I make a run for it before Mr. Groce can arrive, walkie-talkie in hand, and find that it's Aura Ambrose who's just broken free.

9

~

While some "mad geniuses" enjoy great success, many do not. Inspired often, creative nut jobs don't have the focus of mind needed to complete projects. As prolific as van Gogh was, just imagine what he could have accomplished if he hadn't been such a damned fruitcake.

The music is blaring again as I race up the driveway, which means Mom's probably interfering with the Pilkingtons' hangovers. Mrs. Pilkington will be on our porch any minute, banging on the door and slurring her threats. I throw the front door open, stomp down the hall. But as soon as I hit Mom's bedroom doorway, everything I was going to scream at her disappears, like water down a drain.

Mom's painting—I hate, hate, *hate* this expression—like mad. She sounds like she's been jogging, her breath raspy against her throat as she pushes her brush against the paint blobbed on her palette. Mumbling to herself, she spits the occasional "*Fix.* It'll *fix.*"

Canvases that've been painted on and abandoned—some of them halfway gessoed-over—are strewn everywhere, like a stack of paper that's been tossed into the air and allowed to flutter back down to the ground. They lie face-up, face-down, crooked. They've stained the bedspread, and their corners poke into the walls or dresser. Some look like they've been attacked by a tiger, with long thin slices running lengthwise.

The curtains are splotched with paint, too—even handprints, like someone's been held captive here. Like someone's desperately been trying to claw their way out.

Books—textbooks, art books, coffee table editions—lie open and decimated, their torn-out, wadded-up pages dotting the carpet. And at my feet, right there at the toe of my sneaker, is Mom's old portfolio, dusty and frayed. With the music squirming inside my chest, I squat, open the portfolio, and look inside, flipping through the pages of Mom's work—the drawings Mom sent to art schools back when she was applying to colleges. But that was before she ran away from Nell and moved in with Dad, the summer after she graduated from high school. Before she wound up settling for the college here in town.

Pieces, artwork is called. *Pieces* of artwork. But I can't think of the pictures in Mom's portfolio as *pieces* at all. Actually, I think the portfolio ought to be titled *What It Was Like When Mom Was Whole.* I mean, the person who did this, I think as I flip through the pages, the wild colors, the vibrant swirls, nothing shy, nothing tame, nothing backward about any of it—the woman who painted *this* isn't some dandelion seed. She's a lion. And lions don't get tossed about willy-nilly by the wind. *She'll be back*, I tell myself. *You just wait. She'll open her eyes and yawn and growl. And then we'll drown ourselves in champagne to celebrate her return.*

An electric guitar beats its way past my eardrums and works its way deeper into my brain. I realize Mom's got Pink Floyd on the turntable. "Shine On You Crazy Diamond" is turned up too loud for the speakers; notes buzz like killer bees.

I try to go back to the portfolio, which has always amazed me. To think, my own mother was responsible for these strange, fearless images that refuse to be caged by any *-ism.* These works aren't just abstract, or expressionist, or impressionist. They are somehow a blend of all, with odd angles, incongruous details—broad, fanciful strokes of color breaking up blurry, out-of-focus faces that peer out from windows or cafés or cars or moon craters, each setting so ornately detailed that it seems far more like a photograph than something created entirely by hand.

The more I leaf through it, the more her portfolio taunts me. These pictures are telling me *Look, Aura, right now, you're okay, just like she was. But soon, you won't be. Soon, you* will *start to fall to pieces, see? Because even these pieces—this artwork—it doesn't make any sense. That's the schizo mind at work, Aura. Tiny little pieces, shards, fragments—that's all you'll be. Enjoy being whole while you can. It won't last forever.*

"Goddamn it," Mom snaps, yanking the portfolio

from my hands. Her eyes, wild, accuse me of horrible things. "Are you going to get your hammers and bolts?" she screams. "Are you trying to fix me? *Are* you? Who asked you?" She races to the dresser, grabs something off her vanity mirror, and shoves it in my face. The crystal I'd tried to drop in her housedress the other night. "I'm not broker, broking, broke, broke," she says, her mouth twisting as she fights for words.

"Mom—crystals, right?" I blubber. "Just like when I had mono."

Her face ages, like a film on fast-forward. Lines etch themselves beneath her eyes, around her mouth. Her cheeks sink, creating pools of shadow. "You think I'm sick?" she whispers. "I'm *less*?"

"No—that's not—I don't mean—"

Mom tilts her head toward the light, erasing the shadows in her cheeks. Youth pops across her face as quickly as a kernel of popcorn, replacing the hard shell she'd been the moment before. The vacant hollows of her eyes fill. The stranger steps aside to show me the real her, who still lives, so deep down. "You'll understand someday," she informs me, her voice as clear and unclouded as tap water. "When you're grown, you'll understand these things."

Her words zip through me like electricity. She knows exactly what she's saying. The room spins, my stomach churns, my skin burns. Oh, my God—it *is* true. We're just alike.

I shouldn't leave her. I'm not stupid. My brain knows I shouldn't. But my feet are moving, running, like the house is on fire. It's self-preservation that sends me racing. I grab the keys to the Tempo, *got to escape, got to escape for a little while.*

I tell myself that if I have the car, she'll be safer. It guarantees she won't be behind the wheel. Before I leave, I even turn the deadbolt on the front door and lock the sliding glass door in the kitchen. Maybe, I think, *maybe*, like a caged hamster behind the safety of wire walls, she won't be able to figure out how to get out.

And then I'm steering the Tempo, chewing on the inside of my bottom lip, praying I won't get pulled over for the headlight Mom knocked out in the whole mailbox fiasco. Yeah, okay, I shouldn't drive without a license, all right, but it's not like it's brain surgery. It's *driving.* I mean, take a look at the dopes who leave the DMV with licenses sometime. Besides, it's midmorning, and traffic is down to a murmur. Hands at ten and two, seat belt locked, I remind myself it's no different, really, than steering the riding mower. I avoid the main thoroughfares, taking the side streets to Zellers Photography.

"What the hell?" Nell shouts when she sees me. My heart practically shatters, because this is how I wish it could be at home—I want a mother who gets after me for showing up in the middle of a school day, obviously cutting class. I want a mother who puts her hands on her hips and frowns just like Nell, as she shouts, "You'd better get your butt back to school, kid. I'm not tolerating crap like this."

But I shake my head, tears coating my eyes the way

rain hangs onto a car windshield in a downpour. A serving of normalcy isn't really what I've come for—not today. Details, that's what I want. My sneakers squeak as I hurry across the floor. "That picture," I say, pointing at the beach scene—Nell and her daughter in a crumpled heap on the sand. "Where was it taken?"

"Florida," Nell says, eyeing me like I've flipped my freaking lid. The red of shock and embarrassment starts to creep around the base of my throat.

"No, it wasn't," I argue. "I've been to Florida."

Nell chuckles as she falls into the chair behind her desk. "You ditched school to come debate me on Florida. At least you're not boring, I guess. Worst thing you can be in life, boring. Worse even than being selfish."

"What was he like?" I want to know. "Your husband."

Nell sighs. I get tense, because I figure I'm being completely transparent—and because Nell's the kind of person to call me on it. But she just says, "He was brilliant," as straightforward and matter-of-fact as if I'd asked her where she'd gone to college or what her dad had done for a living. "Was going to write the Great American Anti-Novel, or so he called it. Was going to invent a brand-new art form, one that would make guys like Burroughs and Vonnegut scratch their heads and stroke their chins in amazement." Her eyes go distant.

"But he didn't."

"No," Nell whispers, her eyes going all windshield-in-the-rain, too. "He never did. He tried, though."

"So what happened to him?" I ask, even though I know.

I know it, without anyone ever having told me straight out. *Dead* was all anyone had ever said, as if that word answered questions instead of filling a mind up with a hundred new question marks.

"A lot of mentally ill people take their own lives," she says, then bites down on her bottom lip so that it won't wobble, so that her mouth becomes a sort of dam against the sobs that want to break out. My mom's got the same habit.

But *I* don't—my tears, once started, can never be held back. Streams are already rolling down both cheeks when I tell Nell, "Look, I probably won't be back to work again, all right? So don't think anything about it if I don't show up." My voice is thick and low, and full of more history, suddenly, than the wooden floor in Nell's studio. My voice carries every disappointment I've ever felt, and Mom's, too, and even those of a grandfather I've never met, because it's all becoming so clear to me. Generation after generation of madness hits my shoulders like rain made of concrete blocks. It's verifiable, like one of those damned geometry proofs—this disease comes to artists as surely as lung cancer comes to a person who's been smoking three packs a day for thirty years straight.

Because art is a drug. One that destroys the mind, breaks it, leaves it black and withered and useless. And here I've been surrounded by art my whole life. I've got to quit; I've got to get away from it; I've got to run before it swallows me, the way addiction has swallowed two generations of the Pilkingtons.

"Wait. Aura—what do you mean? Are you quitting? What for?" Nell tries. But I'm out the door, away from her photography, away from art, *away,* because I know that someday, if I'm not careful, I'll be standing in front of some white-coat, drugged into a stupor, my arms frozen like tree branches, a trail of slobber falling out between my lips.

"Forget it," I shout back at her, terror racing through my chest. "Forget it, forget it, forget it," even though what I mean is, forget *me.* And I turn away, stomp toward the Tempo, which I rev to life.

I hightail it away from Nell's studio. Slam the car into drive and gun it.

10

~

Family members who care for a schizophrenic are at risk of burnout. Especially family members who are probably going to be just as sick, raving, and nuts as their wacked-out relative.

Mom finally, finally falls asleep around dawn, collapsing onto her bed for the first time in what feels like about three centuries. By a quarter to eight, her snores are so rattle-the-whole-house loud, I figure she's out hard enough to maybe sleep through the entire day. I dress and grab the keys, since I don't have time at this point to walk—and I really do need to put in an appearance at school. *No, nothing wrong at home, Fritz, nothing, just going through my oh-so-cool rebellious phase. Sorry about running out on you yesterday and skipping all my afternoon classes.*

I start to reach for the handle of my canvas bag, stopping short when I realize it's not sitting on the floor beside the kitchen table, but on Jeremy's skateboard. I reach down to touch a rough patch along the edge of the board that maybe got scraped up during some trick. Touch it like I would if it were Jeremy's elbow, wounded in a fall. I close my eyes and let my fingers run along the thick swirls of paint he's smeared across the board, tracing them like the curves and indentions of taut muscles down a stomach. My mind explodes with images I'd paint—*if,* I remind myself, standing and kicking the board into the back corner of the kitchen, painting wasn't like lying down in the middle of the freaking highway, waiting for a semi to turn me into Aura hash.

The defroster in the Tempo is shot, so I drive with the windows cracked—the extra-bitter Missouri October morning makes the whole car feel like a deep-freeze. My breath comes out in opaque puffs that probably make me look like I'm smoking. And I'm such a ball of nerves, trying to make it seem like I'm an expert driver and not someone who's just slipped behind the wheel for the third time in her entire freaking *life*, I really wish I were. Smoking, that is. I wish my lungs were full of smoke right now.

Mr. Groce, King of Crestview Security, doesn't exactly smile upon fifteen-year-olds who are driving illegally, so I pass the entrance to the Crestview lot and head for the nearby Kmart. Cut the engine out behind the Tire & Lube.

By the time I park, though, I realize it's taken me longer to drive to school than it usually does to walk. Criminy.

I've really got to huff it, past the already empty Circle, all the way across the field and through the Crestview High back door.

And smack into a chest as soft as an overstuffed living room chair.

"Badge," the chest barks at me. It belongs to Mr. Groce, who's wearing his usual eighties-vintage brown plaid jacket, purchased when he was six sizes smaller.

I reach into my hoodie and pull out my laminated ID badge on a bright yellow cord. The faculty acts like they're no big deal, like they're just time cards you'd punch any old day at the mind-numbing office. Nobody has the balls to say what they really are: dog tags. If there's ever a Crestview High massacre, Groce will know who to mail my mutilated body to.

Less paperwork that way, you know. Less money spent on those pesky DNA tests.

He glares at me as I try to make a last-second dip into the ladies' room. Before I can even touch the handle, though, he jingles his keys out of his pocket and slams them into the lock. My shoulders droop. I could tell him, *I just have to pee,* but who wants to discuss bodily functions with a fifty-year-old male security guard? Reminds me of having to watch the birds 'n bees video with the hairy-knuckled fifth grade gym teacher. Ultra-creepy. Besides, he's obviously made up his mind about me—I'm *not* a glistening golden, but the bad guy, guilty until proven innocent, a tramp who will light up as soon as I step into the back stall (and probably even start a fire when I toss a still-burning cigarette butt into the trash can). I am just the kind of gypsy scum who will destroy anything her sneaker tread touches—so I don't get to use the cleanest bathroom in the school.

I glare right back as I head for the stairs. I should have known better than to leave the house without using the bathroom. What am I, five?

Ah, well, no time now. I hike the sleeve of my hoodie—8:05. *Damn!* And I take the steps two at a time. My feet echo through the dead stairwell.

By midmorning, I'm not sure why I even bothered coming to school at all. It takes the entirety of first period to straighten everything out with the stupid attendance secretaries, and a bomb threat means the entire student body spends second and third periods out in the parking lot, shivering in the October cold. Since it's Vote for Your Homecoming Queen Bullshit of the Century Day, the glistening goldens wander through the parking lot while we wait for the fire department to give the thumbs-up, smiling at all the rest of us as if to say, *Why, I never thought you were a gypsy in the first place. Want to share my last stick of Juicy Fruit?*

Gag.

Across the lot, I see Janny, alone, arms across her chest. And I walk up to her, a smile plastered on my cheeks like a clown's grin. Because every other fight we've had has ended with me showing up at her house like nothing bad had ever been said between us. Ten minutes after ringing her doorbell, we'd be in front of her TV, passing a bowl of popcorn back and forth, and in the last year or so, every time one of my insurance-selling Dad's retarded commercials came on, Janny would put her head on my shoulder. We'd watch my very own dad put his arm around Brandi, who was holding their daughter, the words *Auto*, *Home*, *Life*, *Health* flashing on the screen with the American Family logo. Janny'd point to my little half-sister and say, "I think Carolyn's a dumb name, anyway."

But now, when I walk up to her, her angry eyes start boring into my forehead. Like a drill bit, you know? Like trepanation. They used to do that to crazies—drill holes right into their skulls to let the demons out.

"What do you want now, Aura?" she asks, annoyed.

"Come on, Janny, you act like I'm Ethan. Like every time you turn around, you have to wipe my ass."

"Frankly, I'm surprised you even remember his name," she spits.

My brain spins. I don't know where this is coming from. "You know, I've got a few things on my mind, Janny. I've got this person at home—remember her? And I don't know what to do, okay? And maybe if somebody helped me *out*—"

"So go find somebody, creep," she says. "I just came today to clean out my locker."

"Clean out your locker," I repeat.

"I moved out, okay? Of my parents' house, all right? And I got a job, because Ace is gone—"

"Wait, wait," I say, reaching for Janny's arm, but she squirms away.

"Yeah, big surprise, right? One thing's for sure—don't ever trust a guy named Ace to come through for you when you find yourself in a jam. Guys named Ace get in their 1966 El Camino street racers and head for the coast. Any coast. And dumb old Janny Jamison couldn't even figure *that* one out. And the thing is," Janny blurts, like she's been waiting eons for the chance to tell someone this very thing, "they say it's the woman's prerogative to change her mind. But that's wrong. Guys are the ones who get to say, 'You know what? I don't want to be with you after all.' They get to say it *after* they've sucked all the sweetness out of you, just like those cheap, liquid-filled wax candy things we used to get for Halloween. They leave you a dried up, empty piece of wax, and head off to find somebody else who still has some sweetness inside."

I clutch my chest. "Janny, I didn't know—"

"No," she says, trying to suck the snot back into her nose. "You didn't. And you didn't bother to find out, either. You're not the only person with problems, Aura. Real, shitty, stupid problems. And I'm sorry, but I can't take on any more. Especially not from someone who just thinks I'm whining about a stuffy nose. Leave me alone, okay? Just leave me the hell alone."

As I watch Janny turn to disappear in the crowd, I find out that when my heart shatters, it sounds just like a glass vase splintering into a million pieces on a tile floor.

I hurry over to the side of the building, away from the

parking lot. And I feel so rotten and so lost and so scared, I'm actually crying. Tears rolling, just like some weepy little baby—like that stupid douche bag Adam Riley, who cried in the first grade when a substitute teacher showed up, because he wasn't supposed to talk to strangers and there was one in his room and he just *had* to get out of there, go to his mommy.

Criminy. I'm crying just like that, and while I'm blubbering, of all the stupid rotten luck, Jeremy Barnes is sitting on the sidewalk by the library exit, looking right at me. He's watching me make a complete and total fool of myself. He's standing up, and he's lunging toward me. He's got his fingers wrapped around my wrist like a handcuff.

I start to wrench myself away, but quit because his fingers are warm, and his touch makes a feverish ache explode through me.

"Come here," he insists, loosening his grip to slide his hand down, weave his fingers between mine—God, like I'm some awful girly-girl, the fact that we're holding hands makes me want to squeal. He tugs me forward, and our feet start smacking the parking lot—his Adidas and my old Converse with the paint all over the toe. We race to the Circle, toward a black Firebird with a fender that's been mangled so long, the dents have actually started to rust.

"Is this yours?" I ask dumbly, my voice still sounding teary, which I hate.

Jeremy shakes his head. "Nope," he says as he smacks the back bumper. The trunk creaks open.

I guess I'm looking at him all horrified, because he

grins, his Cindy Crawford beauty mark wiggling. "Don't worry," he says. "Guy that owns it gives me a ride every morning. And this," he says, pulling a beat-up board from the trunk, "is mine. As of this morning."

"For the—for the necklaces," I say, wiping at my face with the cuff of my hoodie. Because I want him to know I've been paying attention, too. That maybe I've got my own collection of Jeremy factoids.

Jeremy nods. "Couple of hours ago, I figured the saw *was* the best place for this thing. But now—I think maybe she's got one more ride in her."

He slams the trunk shut, and he's got my hand again—his skin is something to savor, like a piece of chocolate on my tongue. He's tugging me down the street, to the corner, where the curb dips down into a concrete drainage ditch. Somebody's spray painted *Thug Life* across the ditch in enormous white letters, and a few brown beer bottles lay scattered in the overgrown grass that separates the curb from the sidewalk.

Jeremy puts the board down against the curb. When he turns to me, his eyes glitter.

"So what?" I say, shoving my hands in the front pocket of my hoodie. "We came out here so I can watch you turn some sort of fancy skating tricks?"

He flashes a half grin and shakes his head.

"Oh, no," I say, staring at the ditch. "That thing must drop off—what—five feet?"

"That's nothing," Jeremy says with a shrug.

"People have broken their necks doing less."

But Jeremy's got my shoulder, and he's pushing me, and my feet are suddenly on top of the board. And he's telling me, "Just let the tip dip forward—easy—like flying."

"No—no," I say, still protesting, because this really doesn't make any sense. "I don't know how—I'll fall," I insist, but he's pushing me, the wheels roll, dip, and I'm gliding, not down, but *deep*. Not *against* the wind, but *into* it. And there's nothing, in this tiny moment—nothing bad, anyway—just the explosion of air in my ears, and the cool pelt of wind that dries the tears from my face. Laughter bubbles out from underneath the concrete blocks of *now*. The whole world just feels so good, so light, so—Jesus. Normal.

I start to lose my balance as the board rides the curve at the bottom of the ditch; my laughter turns to a scream as I wobble. I don't know what it is skaters do to keep their boards flying over the top edges of half-pipes, anyway, so I jump off, let the board rock itself to a stop.

Jeremy calls, "How do you feel now?"

I throw my head back to look up at him, hands in his pockets, smiling at me, so proud of himself.

"Human," I say.

He squats, holds his hand down for me to grab. I tuck his board beneath my arm just before he hoists me back onto the curb. His skin is delicious—I keep clutching his fingers as I let the wheels clatter to the ground. For a minute, as we're standing there staring at each other, I think maybe he's even going to try to kiss me. My heart starts to race, hoping, hoping…

Instead, he pops the skateboard and catches one of the front wheels so that it hangs from his hand crooked, the way a little girl might hold her dolly by one arm. "Now you understand," he says. But before he explains himself, he's already turning away, heading toward the distant throngs in the Crestview parking lot that are all starting to flow back into school.

"Understand what?" I yell. Who the hell does he think he is with all this cryptic shit, some Zen master?

"My *board*, Aura," he calls over his shoulder. "I want my damn board back. Paint my *board*, already." The mere word—paint—makes me feel a little woozy.

As I watch him walk away, desire is like the tides I fought in Florida—like a giant's fist that grabs my body and forces me so far down beneath the surface, I almost doubt I'll ever breathe air again.

By the time I jog back into school, the crackly voice on the intercom is sending us all to our fourth period classes, which, for me, is English. I head into Ol' Lady Kolaite's room like a zombie, my skin on fire because the sweet fix I got from Jeremy's board was fleeting, and the bitter-as-an-unripe-lime taste of my whole stupid life has already exploded in my mouth.

Kolaite kicks the class into gear; in the seat beside me, Katie Pretti tugs her sweater sleeves over her wrists and half-way down her hands, hiding her thumbs. She sighs and leans back, with that look, you know? That look of being tied up, like it's not really her sweater sleeves she's tugged on, but handcuffs. Like she's not the one who put the cuffs on—no, it was some unseen sadistic s.o.b. who kidnapped her out behind the QuikTrip yesterday afternoon when she stopped in for a cherry Icee. Because everybody knows that's what high school really feels like. It's being handcuffed. It's being held against your every last will.

As soon as she sighs, George's hand reaches for her back. He sits one seat behind her, like he does in every class they have together. George, blue-eyed, blond-haired. *Georgy Porgy.* Beautiful and untroubled and smart and light and sweet and easy as a boy in a cheesy '80s TV show—Kirk Cameron or Scott Baio. *Don't worry, man, it'll all work out soon. I mean, it's already 7:49.* George Conyers only kissed one girl, lucky Katie, and *never* made her cry. And the minute he starts to scratch her back, her whole face changes. She's not in jail anymore.

Asinine class couple. Why the hell did I even bother with school today?

I'm just so sick of being around so many people with nothing wrong, *nothing*—they have no clue what it's like to really lose sleep over anything—that suddenly I'm writing again, even though I swore I wouldn't, I wouldn't…

If I had a
cigarette,
I'd smoke it.

If I had a
man,
I'd grope him.

If I had somewhere
to run,
I would fly away.

If I had
tears left,
I'd cry them.

If I had the
reasons,
I'd hoard them.

If I had somewhere
to run,
I would fly away.

If I had a heart,
I'd feed it.
Shelter, nurture,
and protect it.
And in return,
if it made love,

I would fly away…

"Aura? Aura, dear?" It's Mrs. Kolaite, looking at me with this false, put-on worry. I swear, she's applied it to her face like mascara.

"Yes," I say, scooting up in my chair—where'd they get school chairs, anyway? Things might as well be made out of bricks. "I'm following along fine," I blubber, flipping the shiny pages of my textbook back and forth.

Because the thing is, when they're not treating us like gypsy scum, the teachers are all looking at us in this condescending way. I mean, they think we're capable of hacking into the computers to change our grades, and they practically nail their purses to their chests because they think we're crafty enough to sell their identities over the Internet, but they don't think we could ever grasp something as simple as a freaking *metaphor*?

How's this for metaphor, Kolaite? *Sanity is a sonnet with a strict meter and rhyme scheme—and my mind is free verse.*

II

~

Journaling can be useful in keeping track of a schizophrenic family member's behavior. Often, the changes are so slight, families can be caught off-guard by a psychotic break. Journaling can help family members nip said psychotic break in the bud.

"Happy birthday, pretty girl," Brandi coos in her Betty Boop voice as soon as the door flies open. She smothers me with a fakey-poo, sorority-sister-style hug and kiss, then gives me enough room to step inside the downtown loft apartment she shares with Dad and Carolyn.

School's been canceled for some sort of teacher betterment crap, and I can think of about a million things I'd like to do with my free Friday other than coming over here—like, say, putting my head in a vice or getting all of my toenails extracted one by one. But it's my birthday, which means it's time for Dad and Brandi to pretend they can be labeled Really Good People Who Are Hip To Hanging With Keith's *Other* Daughter.

As the door falls shut, Brandi lets out a squeaky "Whew" while she smooths some bottle-blond flyaways toward her ponytail and flashes her enormous neonatal eyes at me. "Caterer just left. I swear, I didn't think he was ever going to get here."

"Caterer?" I say, my feet going cold. "I didn't want some awful party. I told Dad that. Isn't it just *us*?"

Brandi nods. "You, me, Keith, and Carolyn," she agrees. "But how often do you turn sweet sixteen?" She waves a hand at me, shakes her head. Tugs at her blouse as though she's just so frazzled between the baby and the husband and freaking pool boy they probably have for their nauseating whirlpool tub, she couldn't find anything decent to wear. But the truth is, her blouse and skirt smell like the high-end department store I know they came from, and they do an amazing job of showing off her Pilates-toned waist and her dancer's legs.

"Don't know that I'll ever call *that* place again. Not exactly friendly, if you know what I mean," she says as she rolls her ice-blue eyes behind her thick, black mascara.

I want to tell her I'd probably be ticked, too, if I was them—after all, Brandi's the one who just treated some professional catering service like a neighborhood pizza delivery boy. Not that Brandi believes she could ever truly wrong anyone—not even me, or my mother, who was still married to my dad when she arrived on the scene.

"You like curry, right?" Brandi says, shimmying her tight little ass into their kitchen, loaded to the gills with granite countertops, a hand-cut travertine floor, and all the stainless steel appliances that the world says you're supposed to like.

I prefer the thirty-year-old olive refrigerator in the kitchen I share with Mom, actually.

"Hey, sweetie," Dad says as he bursts from a bedroom, a blond and pouty Carolyn on his hip. *Sweetie.* The word's like electricity shooting up my spine. Because it's replaced my real name, since he's too embarrassed to even say it anymore—*Aura,* like it's a tattoo he got when he was eighteen and now hides under long-sleeved shirts, even in August. *Aura,* like it's some silly notion of his misspent youth, something he outgrew.

"I'm afraid we're in a bit of a weepy mood today," Dad says, kissing the top of Carolyn's head, then smoothing her corn-silk bangs.

"Another one of our commercials is on," Brandi yells from the kitchen, pointing to the ridiculous TV in their refrigerator door while she dishes up our lunch of Indian food, which smells a little like gym socks to me. "I really like this one," she says, staring at the small screen. "Have you seen it, Aura?"

Get real.

The only consolation in this whole stupid mess is that I'm sure Brandi's parents hate Dad. And I mean, *hate.* Their baby girl was supposed to marry a CEO, or a Nobel-Prize-winning chemist, or better yet, the president of Outer

Mongolia. Not some stupid old insurance agent with a previous marriage and another child. I figure Thanksgiving's a real bitch for him—imagining it (and the impending divorce that will surely, surely come once Brandi meets said Nobel-Prize-winning chemist) is really the only thing that'll get me through this crummy day.

"Come and get it," Brandi sings, carrying our plates to the table.

I've got two boxes stacked next to my place setting (along with a card containing my obligatory fifty bucks), each professionally gift-wrapped. But I couldn't care less about a couple of crappy presents, not with what I left at home. The words down there in the pit of my stomach—*Mom's a rope raveling down to nothing*—fester like a giant pile of salmonella, making me feel like I'm about to throw up. I want to tell Dad—just blurt it and have it over with. I want to tell *someone,* especially since Janny's no help at all. (And do I blame her? Do I, with everything that's falling on her right now? Yeah, in all honesty, I guess I really do.) But I promised Mom, too—*no meds, no more, not ever again*—and that's exactly what Dad's going to want to do. Tie her arms behind her and shove a funnel in-between her lips, if that's what it takes to get the pills down. And I swore, too, *no Dad.* If I break my promises, I'm terrified Mom will snatch her love away, like it was never truly mine to begin with, but a library book that I'm now supposed to return.

I guess I stare at the presents a long time, thinking all

this, because Brandi says, "Go on—they're yours, you can open them if you want."

"No—I just..." I stutter. "I..." The words try to crawl up, they really do, as I look at Dad, eyes pleading. But he's too busy tying Carolyn's bib on to notice.

It occurs to me, maybe I don't have to say it. Maybe Dad could just see it for himself, right? Kind of accidentally? So I say, "You guys going to bring Carolyn by the house to trick-or-treat this year?"

Dad just looks at me, offended that I've even mentioned his old house. Like I'm bringing up the time he went streaking across the football field when he was a drunk philosophy major out for a teensy bit of fun.

"We're taking her to the club," Brandi says. She bites into something brown and slimy and lets out a "*Mmmmm.*"

"The club? The *country* club?" I say, wrinkling my nose as I look across the table in complete and total disbelief at my dad.

"Carolyn is getting to the age where we can really enjoy the holidays," Brandi says casually. "I actually can't wait until we've got a little tween in the house. I mean, there are just *so* many things to do, once they get old enough," like I'm the fucking next-door neighbor. "And Keith is so good about the holidays. Some men aren't, you know."

This practically lights my whole scalp on fire. "Yeah," I say, glaring at Dad. "Really good. Especially with picking out Christmas trees."

The silence that falls over the table has a pulse. An

actual pulse. Because Dad and I are both thinking about the same thing: that last Christmas, when Keith was still *my* dad, back when I was thirteen years old. Mom had voluntarily gotten on her meds to please him—not another mirage like the one she'd had on the soccer field, and no more running away from home to climb a Colorado mountaintop (the episode that had officially filled the bathroom cabinet with amber bottles). Everything was going so well at home, and stupid me, I actually believed the ground under my feet was solid.

Dad and I split up, each of us racing through the Christmas tree lot that was like a forest that had suddenly come to roost beside an out-of-business gas station. When I found one—not too tall, nice and full—and I knew, *this is it*, I turned to call him.

But he wasn't alone. He was with a woman—blond hair, neonatal eyes, and it was all so obvious it should have had theme music behind it, the score from some sweeping love story. As he tightened Brandi's pink cashmere scarf around her throat, it occurred to me just how much like a lie pine trees smell.

The way they smiled at each other... God, that sickeningly sweet smile. I swear, that look they exchanged, even from the other side of the lot, I could taste it. The back of my tongue actually burned.

I tightened my grip on the neck of the spruce I'd wanted to show him, like I was strangling the thing—like I'd have strangled *him* if I could.

Brandi skittered off across the tree lot like a scared

house cat when she caught me watching them. Of course, I didn't know that was her name—not then, and Dad pretended not to, either.

"Never seen her before," he insisted, clearing his throat repeatedly. "Just a lady who dropped her scarf." And I knew. *Merry fucking Christmas, Aura.*

I stomped off, into the thick of trees, wishing I really were in the midst of a forest and not some parking lot, that I could get turned around in the dense sameness of branches like some kid at a wilderness retreat, and never be heard from again. Because he was changing all the rules, Dad was, and even then, I was wondering about the rule that went something like, *must love Aura.* And I was thinking that maybe he'd revise that one, too. Or cross it off the list completely. *Cross it off the list completely*, I think as I stare at him from the other side of the antique dining table. *Definitely.*

"Yes," Brandi says, ridiculously oblivious to the elephant in the room. How stupid could one woman be? "Keith is really good at picking out gorgeous trees."

"Yeah," I say, tightening the hold on my glare. "A real, chainsawed tree, killed in the name of the jolly good ho-ho-holidays."

"And gifts," Brandi says, winking at Dad.

"Gifts," I snarl, shaking my head. Because the dad who lived with *me* had railed against Christmas, or modern Christmas anyway, screaming about commercialization and how *we* weren't going to be manipulated by an ad campaign. And we never once bought a single gift for each other, never, not in all the years we lived together. Not for Christmas, and not for birthdays, either. Made plenty—but never bought one. Somehow it was always so special, because anybody can get some crummy old sweater, but who else in the history of the world ever got an Ambrose Original?

I'm about to ask him, *Don't you ever remember the way we'd once avoided store-bought presents like the plague?* But Brandi squeaks, "We're actually going to the *Caribbean* for Christmas."

"You're what?"

"Mmm-hmm. Keith's idea," she says, patting Dad's hand. "Tropical paradise. White sands and blue water. It's going to be our new family tradition. To the ocean for Christmas. Someday, when Carolyn's just a *teensy* bit older, we'll all go snorkeling together."

I let my fork clunk against the edge of my plate, feeling like the Ambrose Original has just fallen from the sky to squash me into a pile of bloody guts. "And surfing competitions, too, right?" I say, eyebrow raised. "Riding on the backs of dolphins?"

Dad sighs and glares at me, like I'm doing something rotten on purpose.

"How *is* your mother, Aura?" Brandi asks, like our oh-so-pleasant conversation is just meandering along so delightfully—if, by delightful, what you really mean is an experience that brings to mind descriptions of water torture.

I tense up. "Fine," I say defensively, before I can even stop myself. Before I can realize that my knee-jerk lie is the exact opposite of what I'd really hoped to say. "Fine." What a liar I am. Not that they care. Not that they really want to know.

"Well, eat up," Brandi says, "because I ordered coconut barfi for dessert."

"Coconut barf?" I screech. "What?"

This sends Brandi and Dad into hysterics, which makes me feel like a complete idiot.

"*Burr-fee*," she corrects, through guffaws. "It's like coconut fudge. Instead of some plain old cake."

I'm red in the face, I know it, and Dad's eating my humiliation up like Brandi was shoveling down the Indian food just a second ago.

I can't stand curry—Brandi would know that if she'd paid any attention at all the night she and Dad took me out to announce their sickening engagement. So I reach for my packages instead.

"That one's from me," Brandi says proudly.

I shake the top off the box, peel back the tissue paper, and find a blouse. A designer white blouse.

"You don't like it," Brandi says, disappointed.

"It's fitted," I say, eyeing the seams that curve in at the sides—just the kind of thing that makes my boobs look like watermelons. "I don't wear fitted clothes."

"But, Aura, most girls would *kill* for a figure like yours. Or pay a fortune in plastic surgery for it, anyway."

"My figure is exactly why I never wear clothes like this," I say, shoving it back into the box.

"Well, hon—I can—take it back—"

"No, you won't," Dad barks. "You went to a lot of trouble to shop for Aura, to buy her a shirt that belongs on a lady and not a twelve-year-old boy," he says, eyeing my hoodie. "And I think she'll get plenty of good out of it."

I bite back every word that wants to fly out at him, and reach for Dad's gift. I know what it is before I even open it.

"Journals," I say, shaking the top off the other gift box and peeling back the tissue paper. A whole stack of them.

Some white-coat suggested the journals back when we first put Mom on meds. We. I really mean, *Dad.* A family member was supposed to record her behavior, so we'd know, as the white-coat put it, "if we need to tweak the dosage." Mom was so disgusted, she just glared at him like *tweak this.*

I'd swallowed a laugh and sneaked a glance at Dad, wishing he'd roll his eyes. But he'd changed by then—he'd cut off his ponytail and given me all his old Sex Pistols records. He was cringing every time he saw me leave with Mom for a day of classes at the art museum. He grew red in the face every time he found one of Mom's crystals on the kitchen counter. Dad wasn't the same person who read all of Mom's new-age metaphysics books. He wasn't the guy who'd helped Mom try to hypnotize me, wanting to find out who I'd been in a previous life. He wasn't the guy who'd grounded me for a month after I'd giggled during a séance the three of us had held because Mom had wanted to reconnect with her dead father. That day, in the white-coat's office, Dad was the kind of creep who gobbled that journal bullshit down like a starving eight-year-old with free reign at Mickey D's.

I run my fingers down the corduroy cover on the top journal in the stack. I guess somewhere in his brain, he figures all it takes is a hundred bound, blank sheets to make it okay that he's not around anymore. To make it okay that Mom's all mine. Like, *here we have this pretty little cloth-covered book and now Aura won't be mad at me.* For Dad, parenting has become just like shooting one of his stupid insurance ads—some makeup to cover the blemishes, a flashy smile, and *wham!* He's got himself a regular picture-perfect family.

"So you can keep track of her," Dad says, like he does every single freaking year when he gives me my usual pile of journals. "Write every day, Aura. It's very important."

I nod. The sad truth is, Dad only bothers to think about Mom in the same way anybody in the world thinks about an old flame. You know, once in a blue moon, you might get to remembering them—there you are, stretched out on the back porch on a summer night with the lightning bugs and a nice cold beer, and you say something like, *I wonder what happened to Adam Riley. First boy I ever made out with, back in the ninth grade. He gave me mono, the bastard. I hope he's scrubbing toilets at Wendy's and has a bad case of the clap.*

Yeah, that's how Dad thinks about Mom. Only when that blue moon finds him, he's on the back nine of a golf course, because he figured it out the second time around and married into money. And he's standing there in the bright, warm sun, and he's thinking, *Wonder what that freakazoid first wife of mine is doing with all that alimony she's got me paying out the ass for. Ah, well, at least I was smart enough to have a kid with her so that she'll always be taken care of and all I'll ever have to do is give the kid a pile of journals and sing, "Happy Birthday," loiddy-doiddy-di.*

Brandi wipes her mouth on a white linen napkin and asks, "How'd you get out here today? Did your mom bring you? Because, you know, hon, she could come inside."

And do what? I want to ask. *Wait on the balcony until we're done?*

I shake my head no, but my "no" means I now have to explain how I really did get to the loft. Because dear old Dad hasn't even offered a single driver's lesson. And if I lied and said, *Oh, yeah, Dad, got my license this morning. Me and Mom went right to the DMV and I took my test, and gee-williker-whiz, I passed with flying freaking colors,* then he'd want to see my license. Or Brandi would. So she could *oooh* and *ahhh* all over it while getting that sickeningly pleased look on her face that says she knows she takes a better picture than me.

I get all stiff inside, like the time Dad caught me smoking his Camels in the garage. (I wonder if Dad was honest about once having a pack-a-day habit when he applied for his own health insurance. Probably not. That happened to somebody else. A guy who married a schizo and named his kid after the energy field his wife swore she saw around their newborn daughter's head.) *What the hell do I say?*

"I . . . I took the bus," I lie, praying that Dad hasn't seen the Tempo parked out next to the curb.

But Dad frowns, and already—*Aura, you idiot*—I know where I've slipped up. *His loft overlooks the bus terminal.*

"There isn't a bus that comes through at this time," Dad says. "I mean, not that we take the bus, but being this close and all, you notice—"

"Yeah," I say, getting ready to try on lie #2. "Okay. My boyfriend dropped me off."

And dear old Dad—how I would love to kick his stupid teeth in—he just stares at me, all taken aback and shocked.

"Why does that surprise you?" I snap. "It *surprises* you that I'd actually have a boyfriend?"

"You just have a lot going on, is all," Dad says.

"Yeah, well, don't worry about it. I can take care of Mom and date at the same time," I tell the fake concern he's got plastered on his face.

"It's not that," he stammers. "I just—you're awfully young. To have begun all that, I mean."

"To have *begun*?" And it hits me—Dad doesn't remember the summer before last, how I left the retarded anniversary bash that he (actually, Brandi) had thrown for his in-laws, literally five minutes after I'd shown up, because Janny and I had a double date, her with Ace and me with Adam Riley, that disgustingly picture-perfect blond soccer player with ego oozing out his pores. Yeah, Adam Riley, who I hated, but kept going out with anyway, just so I could hang out with Janny.

And he doesn't remember the day he'd decided to drop by like Mr. Good Dad, flicked on the light in the basement, and found me, Janny, Ace, and Adam playing ridiculous, juvenile make-out games (and there I was, wanting to throw up because Adam was such a creep). Doesn't remember how he just stood there, stuttering in the doorway with my week-late birthday present (yet another stack of journals) in his hand. How Adam jumped to his feet and hightailed it out of the basement, or how Ace and Janny laughed their butts off, Ace screaming, "Go, Adam, go!"

My mind boggles. I mean—he doesn't remember *any* of it?

Adam? I think. *He doesn't remember Adam?*

"What's this boy's name?" Dad asks, looking generally as bewildered and flustered as he would if I'd shown up to this sorry excuse for a birthday party in my birthday suit.

"Adam Riley," I say, head tilted down, glaring up at him through my eyebrows.

"I hope—I hope he's a fine boy, Adam."

"Nope. He just dates me 'cause I have the biggest boobs in the eleventh grade," I grumble, shocked that I've said it out loud. *You never paid any goddamned attention at all, did you? You don't even know who I am.*

"But the, uh, the journals," Dad says, all flustered. "Write down her behavior, her moods, anything that strikes you, anything at all. And if it looks like she's going to have another—"

"Episode," I spit, fuming mad now—*fuming*—finishing Dad's sentences, just like I finish them every single goddamned year.

"Right. If she has an episode—"

Oh, Dad, if only you knew...

"You'll be able to look back in your journal and tell the doctor exactly what's wrong. He'll be able to fix it right away. He'll be able to—"

"Tweak the dosage," we both say in unison.

Yeah, I think, staring at him from across the table, the nasty smell of curry filling the space between us. *Tell it like it is, creep. Just say, "Here you go, Aura. Write everything down so I won't ever have to get involved, not one more time." Say it. Say she's mine. You can't be fucking bothered.*

12

~

Hallucinations are the result of hyped-up, super-sharp senses. It's really almost as though a schizophrenic's brain works too well. Often, auditory hallucinations (voices) drive the schizo to engage in completely terrifying behavior.

As I pull the Tempo into the driveway, I feel light-headed and woozy. Our front door is wide open, and a mountain of tools—shovels and rakes and hedge clippers and trowels and hammers—are all piled on the front porch.

"Mom?" I croak. The curry I gagged down to please Brandi is trying to crawl right up my throat.

As I climb out of the car, everything turns slow-motion—like that moment in a movie when a woman sees her little baby tottering out toward the street and realizes a semi is headed their way.

"*Noooooooo*," the mother shouts, her voice all low and distorted. But the truck comes anyway.

Splat. Her kid is a pile of pink guts. Enter Angela Frieson in her white autopsy coat.

This moment is just like that—slow and agonizing, and even though I can't see her, I know Mom's headed straight for disaster. She's headed straight for a metaphorical semi.

Splat.

"Mom?" My voice cracks. I'm sick. I have a fever and blisters in my throat. That's what it feels like, anyway. I have pancreatitis. I have cancer. I'm *dying*, here.

I navigate my way around the pile of tools and burst into the house. "Mom?" I try again, but the word clings to the roof of my mouth.

In the living room, I find more tools—a sledgehammer lies on the floor like a just-fired gun. I swear, I can almost see smoke curling out of it.

"Oh my God," I say. Melodramatically, my hand flies to my forehead, à la actress in a silent movie. "Oh my God," I repeat, standing there like an idiot as I stare at the hole in the wall. She's smashed right through the drywall, into the wooden frame. The hole looks horrifically permanent, like damage inflicted by a hunting rifle. If I stare long enough, the shadows inside the wall start to look black-red, like fresh blood pouring from a wounded heart. Ohmygodohmygodohmygodohmygod.

"Mom!" I shout it this time.

A gust of wind reaches into the living room and slides its cool hand into mine.

Wind? There shouldn't be wind in the middle of the house, not like this, not like there's a—a what?

An open door?

In the kitchen, the mermaids are all swinging back and forth on their strings. The sliding glass door is wide open.

I lunge outside and nearly collapse with relief. She's here, she's here, and she's in one piece. As I step toward her, trying to figure out how to ask her what this is all about, I realize mud is caked on the knees of her jeans and her face and her arms. She's also wearing Dad's old gardening gloves, the ones Mom and I have always hated because they're as scratchy on the inside as sandpaper. But for some reason that doesn't seem to bother her today. Maybe, I catch myself thinking, it even soothes her. Kind of like when you have poison ivy and everything itches so bad that you pour bleach on your rash, hoping the pain of a chemical burn might bring relief.

"What've you done?" I finally manage to ask.

Mom points to the rose bushes that she'd long ago started watering and pruning and caring for like babies, because Dad (who had always been in charge of the yard work) was killing them. Dad was better at cutting away dead limbs, pulling up unwanted weeds. Better at ripping things apart than keeping them alive. So Mom took over the care of the roses, every fall going through the same painstaking ritual to prepare them for the winter—removing all the fallen leaves that had blown across the yard and collected around the bushes, giving the ground a good soaking before it could freeze, mounding nearly a foot of mulch around each plant. She did such an amazing job that the summer before my seventh-grade year, Mrs. Pilkington tried to get Mom to enter her gorgeous pink blooms in the state fair.

But today, instead of trying to protect them, she's killed them all. Their dirt-covered roots are all sticking up into the fall sunshine. They look like dead dogs, roots like rigor-mortis-infused legs. The holes left in the ground are shallow graves.

"You pulled them up?" I say. "You pulled them all up? But you *loved* them."

"I had to," Mom snaps. "They were crying."

"The bushes?" I say, clutching the base of my throat.

"No," she says, as if I'm completely dense, "the walls. The *walls* were crying. I was trying so hard to work, and the crying—it just—it wouldn't let me. I went to find you, I looked everywhere and I called you, but you were gone. Where were you? I wanted so badly to wait, but they wouldn't let me. I went out in the yard and I called your name and you didn't answer, but the walls were crying, crying, and they wouldn't leave me alone. And you were gone!"

"Okay," I say, tears lodged behind my tonsils. "Okay, Mom."

"I had to," Mom insists. "The walls were crying. Loud. Crying. The roots were trying to break through the walls. I could hear them. And those thorns, Aura. The thorns were so sharp and the bushes were trying to grow right through.

And the walls—I couldn't let them suffer. Could I? I had to help. And I looked for you, but I couldn't find you. Where were you?"

Guilt fizzes and pours over the top of me like I'm a just-opened two liter of Dr Pepper.

"I'm really tired now," Mom says. She looks tired. The kind of tired that saturates. She's dripping with tired.

"It's okay, Mom," I say. "I'm just—so sorry."

"I did good, though, right?" she says. "I fixed it? Did you see how I fixed it?"

I stare at the uprooted bushes, thinking I could still maybe rescue them, replant every single one. But then again, if the bushes upset her so much, maybe we're better off this way.

"Yeah, Mom," I say. "You fixed it." I lead her inside, wash her muddy hands in the sink. After I've dried her off, I get her to stretch out on the living room couch. I prop a pillow under her head, and pull the afghan off the back cushions to cover her up.

"You get some rest," I say, smoothing her hair from her face. "I'll be right outside, cleaning up, if you need me."

"You're a good girl," she says, and for a split second I think I see her there—Grace Ambrose, born April 3, 1970. *She is still alive.* I even think I see something a little like an apology: *I am far away right now but hang on I will come back please Aura you are a good girl you will not make me go down there in the dark bottom of a pill bottle I hate them Aura the chemicals but I love you love you love you.*

But then the murky tides roll in, darkening the depths

of her eyes. "Did I ever tell you about my dad?" she asks. "And how amazing he was? He was a writer, you know, and my own mom had him put *away*. He was my *dad*. He was mine, we were kindred spirits. And my mom, she put him away, someplace where everybody sucked the life out of him. Like bloodletting, only with his soul. They used little soul razors on him until his soul was gone. They *killed* him. *Killed*."

"Shh," I tell her, choking back a sob.

"But I'm going to get away from her," Mom promises. "I'm going to run away to my Keith, and we will—*happily ever after.*"

I pull the blanket up to her chin. "Just rest, okay?"

I grab a box of lawn and leaf trash bags from the garage, along with some hedge clippers, and head outside, where I slide into the gloves Mom dropped on the October ground.

I attack the bush closest to me, using the clippers to snip the limbs into manageable chunks. I drop the clippers and start shoving handfuls of limbs into a trash bag.

"Garbage man won't take that, you know." The voice jumps out at me like fake snakes from a magic store can of peanut brittle.

I yelp, putting a hand to my chest.

"Sorry," Joey says from the opposite side of the fence. "Didn't mean to scare you."

I keep clipping and shoving, hoping he'll go back in the house soon. He doesn't get the hint, though, and watches me like I'm some topless dancer with a mouth-watering pitcher of Bud in my hand. But I'm a little afraid to tell him right out to leave me alone, because I remember Dad's warning. *Steer clear of Joey.* What had Dad known? Why didn't he ever really talk to me?

"Hey, Aura," Joey says, his voice as thick and sweet as Karo Syrup. "If you like yard work so much, you can come over here and help me rake leaves."

"I don't think so, Joey," I growl, infusing the words with plenty of *I hope you realize how much trouble I could cause for you if you don't turn around right now. After all, I'm only sixteen years old, you nasty old perverted drunken druggie.*

I turn back to the bushes, listening as Joey's feet crunch in the opposite direction. Once he's disappeared back inside his house, my stomach finally starts to unwind a little.

But it's impossible to shove these limbs into a trash bag that keeps getting tossed around by the October wind. I need someone to hold the bag open—or, I think, as my eyes settle on a metal trash can behind the Pilkingtons' shed, some*thing* to hold it open. I rush to the back of the yard, hoist myself over the chain link, and reach for the can. But as soon as I start to move it, the inside rattles—*clink, clink*—like a whole room of glasses coming together in a toast. When I pop the lid off, I find whiskey bottles. Two empties, one half-full, one never opened.

My stomach kind of twists, and instantly, I wish I'd never seen them at all. Sure, I could snitch. But who would I snitch to? Whose bottles are they? Joey's mother's, most likely, the way things are looking right now—but with the Pilkingtons, you could never be sure. Obviously, though, it's a hiding place for one of them, and I figure I should do *something*—pour the whiskey out. Or toss the bottles into my yard, get rid of them later that night when no one's watching from the twenty or so windows that fill the back of the Pilkington house. Then maybe the rightful owner of the hooch would think they'd been found out by their lush of a family member. Might even be a way to shame that person into stopping. Head them out to rehab for the 142nd time.

My eyes trail over to the window on the back of my own house—the one that leads straight into the living room, where I tucked Mom in. The uprooted bushes lie just below it, in ugly, frantic-looking piles.

The back door bursts open, and Mom emerges from the house with tubes of red paint in her hands. Starts squirting the acrylic all over the plants, screaming, "Fix, fix it. *Fix.*" As if red paint is all her bushes need to come back to life again.

I've still got the lid to the Pilkingtons' trash can in my hand. I stare down—*two empties, one half-full, one never opened. What are you going to do, Aura?* All my options swarm like the bees that will never again be drawn to the sweet smell of Mom's bushes. But the Pilkingtons' mess is none of my business, is it? I've got my own problems right now.

So I slam the lid back on the trash can, pretend I haven't seen a thing. Rush to grab Mom's arm and haul her back into the house, before anyone can see how bad she is.

13

~

Embarrassing behavior can be dealt with in two ways: (1) Telling your relative what will not be tolerated, and (2) Examining your own attitude about why you are allowing yourself to be such a doormat, humiliated every single time you turn around.

"Where are you going?" I ask when Mom emerges from her room dressed—not showered, but at least dressed, wearing a floppy summer dress that makes her too-skinny body look like a pipe cleaner.

She smiles. "You said I was on vacation till Saturday, right? It's Saturday." She taps the newspaper on the kitchen table, pointing to the date. And for a minute, hope flashes like a just-struck match. I mean, Mom's still keeping in touch with the outside world—so what if she's mostly treating that world like some long-lost friend who moved away years ago? In touch is still in touch... right?

And then I realize what she wants, and a cold drizzle traces a path down my back, like I'm standing underneath an icicle that's started to melt. "You're going to *teach*?"

"I always teach."

"But, Mom—I don't think—you're ready yet. A few more days..."

The corners of Mom's mouth turn up softly and her eyes glisten. "I love you," she tells me. "You're my girl."

"You think I'm that easy?" I ask her.

"I think you're mine. I think you understand. You understand. I need to, okay? I just *need* to."

For the first time in my life, as Mom's eyes are pleading and her hands are clutching mine, I really do understand what it must be like when someone who desperately loves an alcoholic suddenly finds that alcoholic on their knees, begging for the key to the liquor cabinet. *Just a nip. I need it, I need it. I love you. You understand you see me from the inside what it's like you know so don't deny me don't don't.*

Mom flashes a diabolical grin. "When you were born," she tells me, pushing my hair behind my shoulders and smoothing it along the top of my head. "When you were born, you had the clearest eyes and most beautiful dark-blue aura. And I knew I wanted to name you Aura, so that the world would know that you were going to do great things." She kisses my forehead. "You're driving, remember?"

"That's a dirty trick," I tell her. And like a fool, I grab the keys off the wall.

At the museum, I steer Mom past the docents—broke college art majors who guide tours through the halls in order to have enough money for their fan brushes and canvas scrapers and potters' throwing ribs. One of them does a double take, frowning at Mom's summer dress that exposes way too much skin on a cold October morning. "Grace?" he says, in that shaky, unsure, *are you okay* tone I was hoping to avoid.

I steer her into the classroom, where she throws my hand off her shoulder, disgusted. "Sit down," she barks, like a pissed-off Doberman.

I don't want to, but the whole class—this one an even mix of white-hairs and volcanic zits—is staring at us with that awful half-shocked, half-scared look. So I take my seat in the back, where I can watch her, where I can save her if I need to, if she falls completely off that cliff. *But will my arms be enough to hold her weight?* I wonder as I start to gnaw on my bottom lip.

Mom stomps to the front of the room, grabs some blank paper, and comes straight for me. Slams the paper down on the table in front of my chair. "Would have been useful if you'd remembered your sketchbook," she tells me, like we're not related at all. Like she's some mean-ass math teacher, bun on the top of her head, who doesn't give a shit what's going on in my personal life, it's time now to learn the quadratic equation.

What happened to my beautiful blue aura? I want to ask, but the words stick in my throat like splintered chicken bones.

"If you're going to insist on following me around, you have to participate," she says.

"Follow you around," I repeat, because I can't quite believe I've heard her right. And besides, that drawing paper she's put in front of me is poison—I can practically see the skulls and crossbones on the top page. Doesn't she get what she's doing? Doesn't she see how similar we are to the Pilkingtons? Doesn't she realize she's an addict, falling apart at the seams, telling me to start using, too?

Don't you remember your father, the writer? I want to scream. *Don't you wish someone had stopped you from picking up that first paintbrush? Don't you see what art is doing to us?*

Mom pounds the table with her fist, wraps her hand around one of my arms, and hauls me to my feet. "Get out," she tells me, pushing me toward the door.

I try to lock my knees, try to dig the toes of my sneakers into the tile. But Mom's still stronger than I am—I'm really not sure where this strength has come from—and she knocks me through the doorway. "Get out and let me work," she snaps, slamming the door in my face.

I want to throw the door open, come right back, keep an eye on her. But I know that would just be provoking a horrible scene. So I hurry past the docents and head outside to sit beneath the maple, where I can watch Mom through the window.

I'm just sitting down, though, when she sees me. She frowns, grabs the blind, and pulls. My shoulders collapse like a tower of blocks. I'm completely shut out. My forehead falls into my hands.

"You get my board done yet?"

I look up, and my heart takes a nosedive, straight to the core of the earth. Jeremy Barnes. He sits next to me, so close that when the breeze catches his hair, it actually tickles my cheek.

I snort and shake my head, because on a day like today, with who knows what going on behind that window blind, this seems about as romantic as the time Adam Riley smashed our faces together when we were in my basement, all tongue and teeth, making me wonder when it could just be over.

"Your timing sucks," I say, but Jeremy only grins, sending his beauty mark dancing.

"Still working on it? Must be a regular *Mona Lisa* or something. I can't wait to see it."

"Jeremy, I just c—" The rest of the word throws its feet down on my tongue, refusing to come out of my mouth. *Can't.* He has no idea what he's asking me to do. That my life isn't as simple as those necklaces he makes. That some people are actually allergic to the sun.

He scrambles to his feet, crouches low, and starts sneaking up on a bush beside the museum's bricks like he's a cat hunting a squirrel. Then he comes rushing back toward me, his hands cupped one over the other like there's something inside, something fragile that he doesn't want to crush.

"Did you know that butterflies carry dreams on their wings?" he asks as he sits back down beside me, even closer than before, his knee against my thigh, the red maple leaves rustling overhead like the lips of a bunch of gossips. *Jeremy and Aura sittin' in a tree...*

I roll my eyes at him and try to push his hands away—they're only an inch from my nose, and I figure it's some sort of joke, like those playground tricks elementary school boys play on all the girls, tossing bugs into their hair or kicking dirt onto their pristine Mary Janes.

But Jeremy shoves his hands even closer to my face and says, "I'm serious. Go on. Whisper your deepest wish, and this guy'll carry it straight to the gods. Some Native American belief, I think. Come on—how many butterflies you see this time of year? He shouldn't even *be* here right now. He's just been sticking around, waiting for you. I know what that's like," he teases, nudging me with his elbow. "Go on. Make a wish."

Okay, it's corny as hell, I know, but it makes my whole body unwind. The way he's offering, for a minute it's like nothing in my life is unconquerable. Nothing—not even Mom—is really quite so bad after all. So I lean in and shoot a whisper into the spaces between his long, artistic-looking fingers. I tell the butterfly that what I wish the most is that my life could truly, honestly be mind-numbingly normal.

Normal. It's so far gone, I'm not sure I'd actually recognize normal if it rang our doorbell.

When Jeremy opens his hand, a monarch, all black and orange, is standing in the middle of his palm. The butterfly flaps his wings a couple of times before taking off.

I laugh as I watch him fly, my giggles as shiny as bubbles. Jeremy's so close, I can smell the lather and steam of his morning shower. And when I close my eyes again, his mouth brushes mine, but not at all like Adam. No, Jeremy touches me the way you'd touch a fragile, pink crab apple blossom—the way you'd barely caress it, knowing how easily it could tear.

His kiss envelops everything at that moment. I lean forward, reaching for him, wanting him not to pull away, because with his lips on mine, I feel like I really am one of those girls that has room in all her pockets for mistakes. A girl who can have crushes on the wrong guys and break curfew and sneak out at night to hang out with her friends. A girl who really does feel naughty when she lights up, because her mother will smell the cigarette smoke in her clothes and ground her for half a century. A girl who has never, in her whole life, felt lower than the bubble gum on the bottom of her shoe.

But our heads jerk apart when the front door of the museum flies open, banging against the building with the force of TNT.

"Fire!" I can hear Mom scream. "It's a fire! The only way out!"

When I turn, Mom's clutching some ancient, bewildered student by the shoulder of his cardigan sweater, crying, "Go! It's the only way out!"

"A fire?" Jeremy says, staring at the door. "In the museum? Seriously?"

But one of the docents has a watercolor in his hand—orange and red and yellow—and he's shouting at Mom, telling her, "A painting, Grace! One of your student's paintings! That's all!"

"What?" Jeremy asks, squinting at her like he's trying to make sense of it all. Slowly, that squint turns into a grin. A chuckle starts to rattle through his lips. Anger explodes through me, because he's so stupid. *Aura collector*, he'd called himself. Right. Sure. Sounds good, Jeremy saving up all the facts, pressing them into his mind like dried rose petals in a ludicrous book of old-fashioned poetry. I should have known it was all a bunch of bunk.

You don't know anything, you moronic jerk, I feel like screaming. Because for all his supposed Aura collecting, he has no idea how much Mom truly terrifies me. He has no idea that when I look at her, I'm not staring at a person, but a mirror. I'm seeing *me*, exactly as I'll be in the future.

I shove Jeremy away, screaming at him, "Loser. You're a *loser*," because his laughter makes me feel like my heart's in a freaking cheese grater. "Get away from me."

I scramble to my feet like he isn't even a boy at all, but rotten flesh.

"Aura," he says, shaking his head and frowning, squinting at me as though I'm a map he's trying to read.

"Go away. Get *away* from me!" I shout, waving my arms like he's some stray cat I've got to get rid of.

As he starts to back away, his face wearing the same confusion as Mom's students, I rush to the museum door. God, I feel like such an ass, because I haven't been watching her like I should have—I've been outside—what? *Flirting?*

This is all my fault.

14

~

It is important to remember that too much emotion on your part can upset your schizo relative even further. Don't shout, or wail, or cry, or nail the door shut.

I call the attendance secretaries the next few days, pretending to be Mom. *Aura has the stomach flu. No, believe me, you don't want* her *in class.*

But by Wednesday afternoon, voices from Crestview start attacking Mom through our answering machine: "Yes, Ms. Ambrose, ah—this is, ah, Pat Harrison," a songbird voice chirps, "and I am no longer allowed to, ah, simply take a call regarding any more of Aura's absences. I must have a doctor's excuse note on file by tomorrow. If, ah, you don't mind."

Yeah, well, maybe *I* mind.

"Ms. Ambrose, this is Janet Fritz at Crestview High with a matter that needs your immediate attention." She pauses to slurp her soda. "It's in regard to Aura's academic career."

What academic career?

I spend the day playing Mom games, trying to manipulate her into doing everyday things like eating. I make a toasted bacon and peanut butter sandwich (Mom's favorite) and take it to her bedroom, where I tell her I'll mix up some paint for her, only, gee whiz, it sure is taking me a long time to stir it up, and Mom, could you taste that sandwich I made for myself and tell me if I've done it right? And golly, look here, I put in too much white again. Gosh, gosh, Mom, don't worry. I'll get it. Just a minute. And here, could you check this shade, and how's that sandwich, did you try it? Take another bite. What do you think about that maple bacon, and just a little blue, and oh, my! How did this happen? Mom's eaten the whole sandwich. That's okay, though, Mom—don't sweat it. I can make myself another.

Jeez. It's like I'm the girl with the six-month-old, not Janny.

"Here, that shade's still not right," Mom says, shooing me away from her paint cans as she chews the last bite of her sandwich. "Come on, move—I've almost got it. I'm so close now. Don't you get it? I can fix it, Aura, if you'll just get the hell out of my way."

I spring for a pizza that night. I know I shouldn't blow

so much on one meal, especially now that Mom's apparently not going to be teaching anymore and we'll be existing solely on Dad's child support. But Mom hasn't eaten anything but a crummy peanut butter sandwich all day. And seriously—who can resist the smell of a piping hot pepperoni with extra cheese?

Not Grace Ambrose, that's who.

I'm grateful that she eats; it makes me feel a little less like a full-body fist, but I only pick at mine. At this rate, I could probably be the cover model for *Anorexics Digest* in about two more weeks.

I shove the pizza leftovers in the fridge, and as I slump against the sink, I pretend I get a note from one of the pepperonis:

Dear Aura,

Thank you for being kind enough to put us in your Frigidaire. The box of Arm & Hammer is a nice touch. We are glad you are not going to just let us sit around on your countertop for days on end—college kids do that all the time, and we have heard horror stories about cockroaches nibbling on poor pepperonis' heads! Ew!!!!!! Anyhoo, thanks again.

Love,
Peppy

P.S. Can you please go get some other groceries? We are all alone in here! We are so LONELY!!!!!

I'm just tired, that's all. Stay cooped up in the house with a schizo too long, and you begin to wonder who the crazy one really is.

Speaking of which…

I tilt my head to the side, listening. No distant radio, no Mom's voice, no clatter-rattle through the hallway, no music from the turntable, no feet in her bedroom. "Mom?" I whisper, on the off-chance that she's actually asleep. It would be one of life's great rewards if she'd actually, if maybe…

I tiptoe out of the kitchen to find she's collapsed on the living room couch. I just stand there a minute, watching Mom's chest swell and fall. I let the scene soak in like moisturizer on winter-chapped skin.

As I stare at Mom's shoulder, rising with another deep breath, I begin to think that now is the perfect opportunity to get Peppy the note-writing pepperoni some friends.

Keys in hand, I head out into the dark. At a quarter past nine, the sky seems like the cold leftovers of a tofu dinner—congealed and unwanted. But the stars are still sparkling, anyway.

I shift the Tempo into neutral and let it slide down the driveway, afraid of waking Mom. And I catch sight of myself, now that my eyes are adjusting to the darkness, in the rearview. No makeup, my long black hair uncombed, in a hoodie with paint splatters all over it (Mom must have worn it at some point). My whole face is dripping with oil, because I haven't been washing it like I should, and because I've been out of zit-zapping cream for a week.

"Warmed-up vomit," I mumble as I crank the ignition, because that's exactly what I look like.

The whole Price Cutter has this funky green hue when I step inside. Like I'm walking into a bug trap that's going to sauté me at any minute. As I fish my happy homemaker list from the pocket of my jeans, the door behind me slides open. Two boys throw their skateboards down and fly past me, toward the cereal aisle.

The pulse of their wheels on the tile makes me remember Jeremy—and how the smell of sprinklers on a new-mown lawn trickles off him every time the wind forces his long hair to dance. Thinking of Jeremy's kiss gives me honest-to-God goose bumps. But I'm no fool. I don't even have the teeniest sliver of a chance with Jeremy. Especially after the horrible things I said to him. I'm not the kind of girl who gets love—or crushes—or boys with beautiful long hair.

"*Hey*," one of the poor schmucks stuck with the night shift shouts at the skaters. He turns to a couple other poor schmucks in identical white shirts and aprons embroidered with the Price Cutter logo. They stare at each other like, *Who's it going to be? Who's going to go after them? Not me, not me.*

I shake my head and push my cart toward the lettuce. I wish there was some way to make a salad smell like a deep dish pepperoni pizza. Maybe if I fried a chicken breast and put it on top of some greens...

Sack-of-salad is on sale, ninety-nine cents. But the kind Mom likes—the one with the romaine and radicchio—is closer to three. I look back down at my list. I could probably afford it, I think, since I don't have many toiletries listed—just toothpaste. (When was the last time I saw Mom actually brush her teeth, anyway?) And while I'm wondering if I should really spring for it, the expensive salad, the skateboarders fly by like twin funnel clouds.

"Get out of here," a middle-aged guy (probably the night manager) screams.

The kids laugh—like it's the only thing a grocery store's good for, you know? Just playing pranks, just ruffling feathers, just having fun.

"I mean it," the manager barks. "Get *out.*"

I watch them careen outside, and it feels like somebody's grabbed the flesh above my belly button and started to twist. *God,* it'd be heaven if I could be on one of those boards, flying out the door. *You stupid boring grown-ups, I'll never be like you, I am free now, and I will never need a giant metal cart, because I will never have to worry about anyone but myself. Just me and my board, to the ends of the earth, man.*

I rub my head and try to concentrate on the salad—*Hurry and decide, Aura. You've got to make this a fast trip, remember? There's only so much time before Mom wakes up again.* I grab the salad Mom likes, and scratch paper towels off the list. No sense in buying the ninety-nine cent salad if she won't eat it, anyway…

A baby's screaming its head off by the time I steer my cart to a checkout lane. And I mean, wailing. The kind of crying that bounces down every single bone in my spine.

"You know somethin' I don't?" my checkout lady asks. When I finally pull myself away from that sound—that god-awful, ear-drum-attacking wail—there she is, in her big blond hair and green eyeliner, grinning at me like she's either retarded or drunk. She's middle-aged and way too chipper for the graveyard shift, if you ask me.

Her age and her wide-eyed cheer slap me with surprise. Usually managers stick young desperates with the rotten hours. I instantly start to wonder what kind of forty-year-old works nights—maybe somebody who hates what's going on at home. Or maybe somebody with *no one* at home. And it hits me how much like heaven *no one at home* sounds. I hate myself instantly for even thinking it.

"You look like you're stockin' a bomb shelter, honey, or preparin' for a blizzard, what with all these canned goods here."

I try to crack a smile, praying my math has been decent and I've only gotten what I can pay cash for. At least there aren't any other customers standing in line behind me who will huff and puff if I have to tell the checker to take some items back.

Nobody but that baby—*Why doesn't somebody shut him up already?*

I know, from the roughly two-point-three seconds I was a babysitter, looking after a nineteen-month-old girl who lived about a block from my house, this isn't tired crying. Not whining because the baby didn't get a toy they wanted. This is *serious* crying. Hurt crying. Sick crying. And I suddenly wonder—*Who shops with a baby at night, anyway?*

A woman in the checkout lane closest to the door jiggles a baby on her hip. The baby's face is tomato red, his mouth screwed into an open grimace, slobber trailing from his bottom lip.

"He has an earache," the woman keeps apologizing. "Sorry. Sorry. We came to try and find some medicine, didn't we, sugar boy?"

When my chipper checkout lady starts ringing me up—*beep, beep, beep*, here go all my cans over the scanner—the woman with the baby turns around to look at me. Jesus. If the world isn't populated by ten people. There she is, Janny Jamison, bouncing Ethan on her hip.

My hand freezes for a second as we stare at each other. I'm not plopping cans on the conveyor belt, I'm staring at this old face. If I hadn't known better, I might have thought she was older than my checkout lady. From the way Ethan's screaming, I figure the reason Janny looks so rotten is that she's been up with him for days on end. And I feel like such a creep, because there *is* something wrong with him. Obviously.

I wonder, as my eyes go dry from staring, if Janny's going to say something to me—I actually start to get all my hopes boiling over the possibility of a *hello*. I have so much to tell her… about Dad and my birthday, and the bushes Mom yanked, and Jeremy. God, even Nell. Janny doesn't know about me working at the studio—because I always thought there'd be more time, a *right* time to tell her about my grandmother. And there are so many things I'm not sure I'm handling right, and if only I could just say them out loud, maybe some of it would make sense. But Janny just turns away, like she's fascinated by whatever her checkout lady's telling her. Like it's some great motherly secret that Janny hasn't clued into yet.

She grabs her plastic shopping bag of over-the-counter medicine and her change. Her back gets as stiff as a ladder as she sprints for the door.

As I'm watching her go, I tell myself I'd better get my hiney back to school tomorrow. I've probably missed at least one quiz and who knows how many assignments, and I've got so much work to do, I feel as backed up as the thirty-year-old garbage disposal in my kitchen sink. And I sure don't want to be a dropout, not like Janny, no way.

"Ma'am?" the checkout lady says. "Ma'am? Anything else?"

Because I feel like the whole world is against me, and if only I could get half a break or just something, *anything* to make me feel better for a minute, I say, "Yeah. Pack of lights." I point at the cigarette display, confident that she'll never ask to see my ID, which I don't have, anyway. She'd never guess I'm as young as I am. I mean, what sixteen-year-old would be caught looking like me, out buying groceries when everyone else who goes to Crestview is probably getting ready to hit the hay? I sure don't look like the future. I don't even look present. I look like the dried-up past.

Sure enough, she pulls down a pack and scans it into my total.

15

~

Schizophrenics have abnormalities of left or right brain functioning. The left brain (the center of logic) seems to be most affected. Which means the right side, the creative side, takes over. And that's why a schizophrenic is like a child playing dress-up, afraid of monsters, living in a world of make-believe.

The next few days, our answering machine is so busy it practically has smoke coming out of it.

"Yes, ah—this is, ah, Pat Harrison," an increasingly familiar songbird voice chirps. "And as I stated before, I am no longer allowed to, ah, simply take a call regarding any more of Aura's absences. I will have to turn the matter over to our, ah, vice principal if I do not see you, Mrs. ah, Ambrose, in, well, I have to see you in person to discuss the matter. Ah, today."

"Ms. Ambrose? This is Janet Fritz, just touching base.

My afternoon is free, and we really do have to discuss this schedule—"

"Yes, this is Mr. Mitchells, the vice principal at Crestview. We've got a disciplinary problem regarding one—let's see—Aura? Ambrose. We've got to straighten this out, okay?"

"This is, ah, well, Pat, ah, Harrison again. I notice that Aura still has not checked in to class today and I just—"

A cartoonish sound explodes—something like a spring breaking, twanging, and I rush down the hall, my heart sick of being asked to beat this hard.

"Hammers!" Mom screams. "Those hammers are going straight into my *head*!"

Again, a spring *boings*. I pick up the pace, jogging into the living room.

Mom's thrown every single music book we ever bought into the middle of the floor. She's got the top popped on the Ambrose Original, and her fingers, completely covered in yellow paint, are making terrible streaks where she touches the piano. Clumsy yellow blotches are ruining her gorgeous painting.

Anger is a blowtorch in my gut. I watch, horrified, as Mom pulls her head from the Ambrose Original, picks up a pair of tree lobbers, and dips them inside the guts. She snips, and another spring snaps. Only they're not springs that are breaking at all, they're *strings*. She's cutting all the strings, screaming, "Putting those hammers straight through my head!"

"*Mom*," I screech, instantly furious because she's destroying the last thing I ever shared with my dad, the last time I was even his. I wrench the lobbers away from her and grab her arms. "Stop!" I shout. "No one's playing it." I'm shaking her—God, like she's some *ketchup bottle,* and if I squeeze hard enough, her insanity will pour out. "Listen to me! I mean it—stop!"

Mom wiggles away from me, grimaces, and covers her ears with her hands, as if to prove me wrong. "Hammers," she moans. "Those hammers are going straight through my head!"

"You're sick!" I bark, because I know that word, more than anything, will hurt her. *Sick* is a knife that digs straight into her flesh, that tears her apart, that doesn't just wound her, it kills her. "Sick!" I scream again, mad enough to slap her—I swear, just slap her, beat her, and I will—I'll hit her if I don't get out of the room.

So I race away, trying to climb back down from the insane high of my anger. In the garage, I slam the lobbers into a space below the workbench, hide them behind an old carpet steamer and a leaf blower.

I swallow air in deep, steady gulps. I breathe so evenly you'd think I was trying to rid myself of the hiccups. Finally, my heart begins to slow down some. But my hands still tremble.

Slowly—timidly, almost—I step back into the kitchen, already feeling horrible for the things I've said to Mom. I know she can't help it. She can't—and I've probably just made everything worse with my outbreak. So I decide to try to make it up to her with food.

Our giant aluminum soup pot bangs against the cabinet

door as I pull it out. Flour, salt, and I let a chuck roast sear while I turn to chopping up an onion—enormous white circles that will turn translucent in the heat before they caramelize.

As I'm chopping, I hear the outside faucet squeal to life. *Is she trying to water the rose bushes?* I wonder. *The same rose bushes she already yanked right out of the ground? Does she still see them? Think they're in full freaking bloom?*

But I don't go outside, because the roast is crackling a warning not to leave it alone. The onions are strong—it's like I'm trying to pierce my eyeballs, the fumes are so sharp. And while I'm chopping, I remember that onions were a freaking dollar and a half a pound the last time I was at the supermarket, and baby carrots were two-fifty a bag. So I'm probably going to use almost two dollars' worth of vegetables in the roast. Not that I guess that sounds like a lot, really—I mean, two bucks. Get in the real world, Ambrose. Two dollars is just a down payment on a tube of cheapie Walgreens lipstick.

Thinking about money makes me wonder about the utility bill—when it comes, or if it's already due this month. I wonder if anyone would know if I forged a check for Mom. Nausea starts to break in waves as I think, *Would I really need to do that? Is she really so bad off she wouldn't be able to fill out a check?*

The pipes continue to hum, making me envision numbers clicking away on our meter, tallying up all the drops of water we've used. I'm suddenly somebody's grumpy old dad—the kind that's always barking about turning off the lights and shutting the door to keep from letting all the heat out.

"Mom," I shout as turn my back on the stove—*Just for a second,* I think—and throw the back door open. I'm mad enough to scold her again, even though I shouldn't. I should just back off, it's such a silly thing, some water trickling out a hose—but I'm ready to really get after her. *Mom, do you think money grows on trees it doesn't it comes from Dad that's the only place now because who would ever let you come back to the museum? So you'd better turn that faucet off right now right now...*

But there's no one to hear.

And I don't mean that in some poetic, metaphorical way, either. I don't mean I'm staring at Mom right now and she's so distant she makes me remember Florida postcards, *wish you were here*. I mean literally *there is no one to hear.* The hose is like a dead snake in the grass—a snake that Angela Frieson got her hands on and decapitated, wanting to know what's inside. Water spills onto the lawn like blood.

I rush to crank the water off.

"Mom?" I shout, scanning our backyard. "Mom!"

I run toward the back fence, where the trees are all overgrown because Dad was the one who knew how to work our chainsaw. He was the one who put that burn bin in the center of the backyard—made it out of chicken wire—and tossed everything he trimmed into it. Burned every last bit of our unwanted waste. And because Mom would rather use her money for brushes, acrylics, oils, pastels, watercolors, pencils, we've never really been able to afford a tree service to step in where Dad left off—not even the guys who drive through neighborhoods with second-hand trailers hitched to the backs of their trucks, knocking on doors and taking any kind of work they can manage to get. The evergreens along the back fence are wild and unruly—*schizo*, that's how the trees look.

"Mom!" I scream again, checking behind the old shed where we still keep our lawn mower and our snow shovel and the tent we never went camping in. But there's no one—and the latch on the back gate has been lifted. *The back gate is open.*

I sprint through the back door and lunge for the roast with a pair of tongs. I flip the giant hunk of meat and sigh. It hasn't burned yet. Almost. But I've saved it. *At least that's one thing I can save,* I find myself thinking. Dinner aromas explode through the kitchen, but Mom's not here to smell them. They can't tickle Mom's nose, because *I don't know where Mom is.*

My whole body feels rubbery—like there's nothing inside that's firm. I could take my arm and push the sides of it together like it's the hose outside. Like there are no bones in me at all.

I throw the roast in the oven and turn to grab the car keys.

As I back down the driveway, I feel like I'm trying to do a balance beam gymnastics routine on a long butcher's knife. It'd be useless to pray my feet won't get cut, because

I know they will. They're bound to. Good God, Grace Ambrose has just disappeared.

Mom, don't do this to me.

My short fingernails don't offer much to chew on, so I bite off a cuticle. It bleeds, but I'd gladly take ten thousand times worse, if it would only mean I could *find* her.

"Don't drive too fast," I scold myself, like I'm a short-tempered driver's ed teacher. Hands at ten and two, I head north on National Street, trying to stay calm. But inside I'm screaming, I'm terrified. I've let her wander away, just like a really bad babysitter who loses a kid at the mall because she's too busy picking out a new bracelet at one of those kiosks to pay attention.

"The museum," I whisper, suddenly sure where I should look. I veer into the turn lane a mere three blocks from our house. But all I'm thinking of is Mom—I imagine her trespassing through backyards and having near-misses with the grills of SUVs on the side streets she'd have to cross in her shortcut—so I don't realize I'm cutting off a guy in a Jeep who blares his horn at me. I cringe and try to wave an apology in the rearview, but he's pissed, like I guess he should be, and while I'm waiting for the signal to turn, he passes me by, screaming at me and flipping me off.

I wave and smile, cussing under my breath. Got to be more careful. Just got to watch it.

As I'm on the edge of my bucket seat, waiting for the green to pop in the turn lane, I keep staring at the *it* that the city insists *has* to be art—the awful, ridiculous sculpture on the corner, the giant pile of bright yellow metal sticks. Yellow like road signs that warn of approaching dangers—sharp curves and slippery streets and school crossings. When I look at it, as much as I don't want to, I think, *Caution, broken pile of Grace up ahead. Detour now.*

Yeah, I'd like to, I'll admit, but I can't—I *can't* detour, I can't just steer around her and go on my way, happy as a freaking lark. I have to go get her. I have to find her and collect the pieces and try to put them into something like order.

I careen into the museum parking lot—I don't mean to, but I make the tires squeal.

Mom's here. In that little park behind the museum, sitting cross-legged in the middle of the grass. I'm relieved to find her, but finding her presents a whole new wad of problems. I mean, she's not some lost and found little kid. Something's led her out here—some shadow, some lie, some hallucination that she thinks is real—and can I really convince her that it's not? Or will she fight me, scream and carry on so that the curator will hear it from her office and call the police, have her hauled away?

My mouth burns, it's so dry. Mom's sitting in front of the outdoor theater made of stone—the one I'd been sketching the day Jeremy gave me his board.

In better times, Mom and I spent our summer evenings here. As soon as she'd wrapped up her last class of the day, we'd walk right out of the museum and head toward that stage, for free concerts or pottery showcases. Once, we even stayed for Shakespeare in the Park—*A Midsummer Night's Dream.* Mom was okay then; her hair was floating in the

July breeze, and she was so beautiful—all fleshy and curvy and strong, in her sleeveless top and her jeans, sandals in the grass beside her and her toes painted a rosy pink. She knew the difference, that summer, between the actors onstage and the people around her who'd started gathering up their blankets and lawn chairs in the middle of the play.

"Where do you think you're going?" Mom shouted at them. "The play's not *over*. Haven't you been paying attention? It's only intermission."

Yeah, that's the Mom I want—that's who I *really* wish I could find. But when I get to her side, it's like that freaky Angela Frieson has gotten there before me, and she's gutted Mom. Emptiness, that's all I see when she looks at me.

"Mom," I say, wiping my eyes. "I've got a pot roast in the oven, so we'd better get back. Aren't you going to be hungry? Don't you want a nice dinner?"

I grab Mom's wrist and try to pull her to her feet, but she brushes me away. "Don't," she says, pointing at the stage. "It's only intermission."

"No—no, Mom, this is an episode," I tell her softly, trying again to use Dad's word, just like I had on the bleachers after my middle school soccer game.

But this time, she frowns at me, shakes her head. "Stop trying to fool me, Aura. It's not funny, you know, making fun of me, fun like that. It's a *play*, obviously."

I collapse on my knees beside her, put my face in my hands.

"Don't worry, Aura," she says, patting my knee. "It always works out in the end."

And that just makes the tears come, as quiet and big as the drops in a summer rainstorm. I turn my face from her so she can't see.

The thing is, it *doesn't* always work out—not even on the stage. Not even on the big screen. I mean, I've watched plenty of late-night horror movies over at Janny's house. And I know that before the heroine finally offs the serial killer, he's already whacked a couple dozen girls and left them rotting by the roadside. Not everybody's the heroine, you know. Some of us just have bit parts in somebody else's story.

I'm terrified that the next time Mom needs me, I'm going to crack right in two. Because the longer this drama goes on, the more I feel like somebody that's going to get offed in Mom's journey. Maybe not *literally* dead, but a spiritual corpse, you know? I'll snap, and the *me* I've always known will be gone, never to emerge again.

And then what?

Then Angela Frieson will get her hands on me earlier than I thought.

16

~

When a loved one is immersed in a schizophrenic episode, you will find yourself unable to think about anything else. Anything. Else.

Who the hell am I kidding? I think the next morning, as I pull the Tempo next to the Crestview High curb. A stream of cars honk, angry, as they all veer around me and pull into the parking lot. Me with my pink schoolgirl sweater, like everything is just fine, the only thing that keeps me up at night is my complexion, loiddy-doiddy-di.

What am I going to say to the attendance secretaries? Or Mr. Mitchells, the vice principal that I've never even seen before in my entire life? Or Kolaite? Or *Fritz*? Is anyone really going to believe I had the stomach flu? Will a note I scribbled myself, hunched over the kitchen counter this morning, be enough for them to just send me on up to Bio II? At this point, would they even believe me if I sauntered in through the front door with an IV on wheels and my own personal nurse to monitor me because I'd been infected with the world's worst case of E. coli, details to be seen on the news at six?

Fritz is going to call me to her office, and I'm going to get reamed. She's going to practically put an ankle bracelet on me, like people wear when they're on house arrest.

I mean, that's the kind of bull that goes on in American high schools. Kid has pot in his locker two doors down from me, but Fritz'll come down on *me*, because I'm not six-foot-three, and I didn't spend the year before in the Brailly Alternative School, which is where all the violent kids get sent in between their stints in juvie. I'm not scary, so I get picked on.

And teachers act like only kids can be bullies.

I'm sure that if anybody knew what was going on—counselors A–Z and the vice principal and Ol' Lady Kolaite and even Dear Abby herself—they'd tilt their heads and wrinkle their eyebrows and plead, *Tell someone, Aura. Tell someone what you're going through. Tell someone how bad your mother is. Get help, get help.* Like there's some sort of twelve step program Mom can go through and *whoopee!* No more schizo.

And then, when they're all in private, like in the middle of the faculty lounge—that off-limits-to-gypsies room that consistently sends the bitter smell of coffee dregs into the hall—they'd all say something completely different. I can just picture Fritz holding my sketch of Ol' Lady Kolaite's face while the rest of the Crestview faculty settle into ancient Naugahyde chairs and shake their heads over that poor, poor Aura Ambrose.

Her mother is crazy, you know.

Yes, yes, I heard. She tried to keep it from us all. Very sneaky girl.

Such a pity, that one.

Yes, well, you know what they say about apples. Never do fall far.

I saw a movie once about a schizo.

We've all seen movies about schizos.

They're dangerous people, you know. The one in my movie, he killed someone in self-defense, or so he claimed—except it wasn't self-defense, because there really was no danger, he was just—

Imagining it all?

Right. Imagining the threat. So he killed this person just because he was paranoid, see?

Yes, yes—what if this girl is paranoid?

We could have another Columbine on our hands, you know.

The best way to monitor her is to put her in a bunch of art classes. Get her to put down on paper what's floating around up there in her mind.

Right—like art therapy. Get her to put it all on paper.

Easier to justify an expulsion that way.

Right.

And can you believe she bought the whole thing about us wanting to put her in the accelerated arts and letters program because she's "talented?" Puh-lease!

And while I'm at it, how do I think I'm going to get through the whole day? Do I really think that I'll be able to leave Mom alone for eight solid hours? Isn't that a little like putting a dog in the backyard with the gate wide open, and expecting her to still be rooted in the exact same spot, just like a good little girl, when you get home from work?

God, I wish I could just shut the door on her and head out into another part of my life. Yeah, I wish I could turn my whole stupid, stinking life into a giant chest of drawers. One compartment for Mom, one compartment for long-lost friends (make that *friend,* singular), one for Dad and his new family, one for the complete and total malarkey that the world likes to call high school. I'd be so careful to make sure nothing in one drawer got misplaced in another—because it would be utter disaster, like if the material from your undershorts and your sports socks could somehow create a bomb just by touching. Put one pair of panties in the wrong drawer and *blam!* The entire house is blown to smithereens.

Blam!

A knock on the passenger's side window makes me jump so hard, my head whacks the roof of the car. I'd gotten so wrapped up in my own thoughts, I hadn't realized that the tardy bell had sounded.

Everyone's already gone inside, and here I am, the Tempo still idling at the curb. I'm right where I pulled over, staring at Crestview like a peeping Tom, trying to decide if I'm really going to head on over to what is becoming my usual space at Kmart two blocks south.

It's Mr. Groce, Security God, glaring at me through the window like he's discovered a machine gun in a violin case that I've been carrying to school for three days. So I lean across the passenger's seat and roll down the window, trying to look as innocent as possible—blink the eyelashes, smear a weepy expression across my face. *Will it work?*

"What's your business here?" Groce growls.

It doesn't. Figures.

"My business?" I chirp.

"Crestview High students are all inside their classrooms. Visitors are required to obtain a pass from the office. And since you don't have a Springfield Public School parking sticker displayed prominently in your windshield, I have to assume you *are* a visitor. No loitering is permitted on school grounds."

I nod.

"*Ever*," he adds.

I realize he's not joking or being smart—he really doesn't know who I am. He's forgotten all about me. So I put the Tempo in drive and take off. But less than a block away, I have to pull over again because I'm laughing so hard. Earlier this month, I was a student. Gypsy scum that Groce personally locked out of the cleanest bathroom in the school. This morning, I'm a security threat.

Another knock—this time on the driver's side window—makes me choke on my own laughter.

"What *now*," I start, and when I turn to look, I can't believe it, of all the rotten luck. Janny Jamison, out for a walk with her kid. I am just so not in the mood for another confrontation.

"You didn't go in," she says, when I finally roll the window down.

"What?" I ask, like an idiot.

"You didn't go into school," Janny says again.

"So?"

"So—how bad is she now? Your mom? Is she getting worse?"

"What, you care all of a sudden?"

"Look, don't try to pretend I didn't see you at the grocery store in the middle of the night, all right? Don't pretend I wasn't at your house watching your mom try to spin the world *backward*."

And if life could ever really be a chest of drawers, Janny's just knocked it over, letting all my undergarments—my horrendously private things—start blowing out in the open. I want her to shut up. I want her not to know so much. Because instead of helping me, all she's doing is showing me everything I'm screwing up.

"You should be in school, Aura."

"And look at you, Ms. Teen Mom USA," I snap. "The picture of scholarship yourself."

Janny doesn't get peeved like I expect her to. She doesn't tell me what a bitch I am or that I can just go rot in my own miserable hell, if that's what I want. She doesn't tell me to piss off, like she told all those boys along the Florida coast when they teased us and called us lesbos because we still held hands like a couple of babies. She just gets this disappointed look on her dishwasher-worn face. You know, that *motherly disappointment.* It's the worst.

"Look, Aura. I gotta take care of him," she says, pointing at her son, who I guess got over his ear infection, because even though he's still all squirmy in his stroller, he's at least not screaming his head off. "I *got* to, all right? That's my job. I'm his mom, right? That's what I do. I spend all day wiping his nose and changing nasty diapers and burping him, because that's what I signed up for. Maybe I didn't mean to—maybe I signed up on accident, but that's what I got now, okay?"

"So?"

"So, I'm telling you, after all I've gone through for him—after all I *still* go through, being a single mom and all, and all I'm bound to go through—I don't want this kid to give up his life for anything. I sure as hell wouldn't stand for him to give up on an education so he could stay home and wipe my ass. I'd just rather slit my wrists, is all."

"Poetic," I say through a glare.

"What are you waiting for, Aura? You waiting for her to try to hurt herself? Are you? You waiting for her to commit suicide, Aura?"

"*Janny*!" I scream. My mouth flaps like a broken screen door, I'm so offended.

"Look, I've been getting on the Internet at the library, and one in ten schizophrenics kill themselves, okay, so—"

"You think I don't know the numbers?" I snap at her.

"Aura, I'm just saying—"

But I can't stand to listen. Not to one more syllable. So I hit the gas and take off again.

17

~

Families who have been through a psychotic episode warn that no amount of preparation can protect you from the shock, panic, and full-body sickening dread you feel when your loved one enters this stage of schizophrenia.

Goddamn you, Janny, I think as I smash the cigarette lighter into the dash. *Why the hell are you acting like you actually care? It was too much, remember?* I tear a cigarette out of the pack, shocked that only two more are left.

Too much, too much—the words bounce around inside my head as I suck at my cigarette—I'm like a vampire with the thing, devouring every last drop of blood from my latest victim. *Yeah, too much, you said, so you ran to your precious Ace. You made your choice—why shove your face back in my business now?*

I slam the car into park and stomp inside, anger rolling off me like steam from the nearby city power plant.

But when I open the front door, everything changes. No more Janny, no more anger, no more smell of cigarette smoke rolling out of my pink schoolgirl sweater. No more Groce, no more Fritz. It's like I've entered another dimension, you know? A dimension that smells of fear and sweat, and it's too hot and too cold and too quiet, and the instant I step into the front hall, the overwhelming silence gives way.

My ears throb against a horrendous squeal that sounds just like a note struck high on the neck of an electric guitar, then sent out of tune with the whammy bar. The note whines, it wails, and I'm thinking of Mom's record player. My first thought is that it's some guitar solo that's attacking my ears. Music that'll have Mrs. Pilkington on our front porch, threatening us yet again with the cops.

But just as I'm about to make a run for Mom's bedroom, to snap that turntable off, the squeal acts like the sound version of a kaleidoscope, because it shifts, it changes color. And I know this isn't music. It's the smoke alarm.

Black curls—like hair caught on a breeze—waft down the front hall and up my nose, crawl inside my head. As the smoke slides down my throat, I cough against it, fighting to breathe. Had I really been sucking this crap into my lungs on purpose just a minute ago? Did I really think it made me feel *better*?

My whole body feels wobbly. Electricity is chewing on my arms. Something's burning. Something's on fire.

My breath is ragged and it scrubs against my lungs like sandpaper as I rush down the hall. What the hell is going on here? Is the whole *house* on fire?

"Mom!" I scream, not sure which direction to turn. From the center of the living room, I can see through the doorway to the kitchen, where the chairs are turned over on their sides. A few of the mermaids lie scattered across the table, and the fishing lines they'd once dangled from hang from the ceiling, broken. One mermaid lies on the floor, her tiny arm reaching out across the linoleum as though asking to be saved.

The scene makes me so queasy, it's like I'm not even in control of my body anymore. It's like I've just come home to find my family slaughtered, and the gruesome sight has sent me into shock.

"Aura!" Mom calls, running into the living room. But she doesn't stop when she gets to my side. Instead, she tackles me, pushing me straight into the kitchen, where she forces me down to the cold floor. My sweaty palm adheres to the linoleum.

"Look," she says, making a motion with her head toward the remaining mermaids that still dangle from the popcorn ceiling. "Look at them, up there, smug. Look what they're doing. Trying to drown me, Aura. See them, how they're swimming, mean, on the surface of the water? How they're making a wall, see? And they won't let me through? Red Rover, Red Rover, like a game, Aura. Send Gracie right over. And every time I try to break their chain, they laugh. Like they think it's some funny game, playground, laughing, and here I am and I'll die and you will, too, now that you're here we'll die this way, see?"

"What's burning, Mom?" I ask, struggling to get away from her. But her hand is like the old vice Dad left behind in the garage, on his workbench. "What's on fire?"

"They're killing us, Aura, killing us," Mom says. "We've got to kill them back first." Her eyes are as wild as a rabid dog's. But the thing is, you're not supposed to run from a dog. That just makes them think you're scared, right? That they've got you cornered? So I reach up to pet her hair. *Nice doggy…*

"You're right, Mom," I say. My body could be what's making the smoke alarm go off, the way it burns. But I can't let her see how terrified I am. "Show me where you're killing them."

"Shh," she scolds me, putting a finger to her lip, like she's afraid they'll overhear. "The tilty floor didn't work. I fixed it, but nothing changed. So I covered it up, and that made them mad. They chased me," she whispers, "into the bathroom."

The ear-shredding screech of the smoke alarm gets louder as I make my way through the living room, toward the hallway that leads to all the bedrooms. That wail is the same pitch and decibel as the fear that courses through my veins, and I can't take it. I just can't—so I jump, swing my hand over my head. I miss, so I try again, this time striking it dead center, where the 9-volt lies. The alarm lets out a weird, lower-pitched yelp, like I've actually hurt it. I hit it a couple more times until it finally breaks.

The plastic shell on the alarm shatters, like a whiskey bottle. A bottle that I could have emptied, taken care of. *You moron. You had a choice. You had a chance, you could have said something, told anyone. You're worthless. You let this happen to her. She's been in here suffering, and you did nothing.*

The fingers that destroyed the smoke alarm sting like they've been stuck with about a hundred carpet nails as I lunge into the bathroom. The bath mat is on fire—it's like some crazy burning bush there in the middle of the floor. Thank God for the tile, which must be made out of the same scorch-proof crap that Dad installed on the backsplash in the kitchen. But the flames are getting dangerously close to the shower curtain—an orange shoot looks like a tongue trying to lick an ice cream cone just out of reach.

I grab a towel off the rack—one of those fluffy, guests-only items that was purchased once-upon-a-time, when there was still a dad and a hope that our house could be honest-to-God normal, with doilies on the arms of La-Z-Boys and extra toothbrushes in the medicine cabinet and a different out-of-state relative on the doorstep each weekend.

I draw the thick towel behind my shoulder and throw it down, over and over, like I've actually got a baseball bat in my hands instead of a floppy piece of material. I attack the fire, beating it, like the flames are the only monster in the house. I beat it as though, once it's dead, this whole situation will be over, and I'll be able to collapse into a sigh of relief.

But once the mat is just a black, charred spot on the

floor, my nose explodes with the firecracker-type stench of a match striking. I look behind me, and Mom's tossing a lit match into the sink where she's piled a few of the mermaids. She's got some newspapers twisted into wicks, too, like kindling in a fireplace. She just keeps lighting and tossing.

"I had them burning awhile, once," she tells me. "They tried to catch me, drag me under. I had them. But the burn is hard to keep, like secrets. Come on, Aura, help me! We've got to kill them before they drown us."

As she tosses another match into the sink, I catch my reflection in the mirror. The details are so sharp—so magnified. I can see every oil-oozing pore. Crooked black eyeliner. The top curve of a red, chapped lip. My faults pile one on top of each other.

Mom just keeps striking match after match, tossing them so wildly that only some wind up in the sink. Others drift scarily close to the washcloths stacked next to our old cracked ceramic toothbrush holder, or fall to the floor.

I'm dancing, even though my stomach is full of rotten pea soup. I'm hopping and jumping and trying to put out all of the matches that tumble, like orange rose petals, to the tile. But I've just stomped one when two more tumble. Four more fall when I get those extinguished. She's in a rhythm, striking them faster, faster. They're burning Mom's bare feet, they're catching the hem of her jeans on fire, and I'm stomping, I'm grabbing those washcloths and beating those flames on the edge of her jeans while the smoke pours from the sink, because the fire has caught on a piece of newspaper, and it's starting to singe one of the mermaids.

The smell of the smoke that trickles off the painted mermaid is acrid, chemical, sick.

"Come on," Mom grumbles as she lights and tosses. "Hurry—hurry!" she screams, like she's seeing the mermaids in the sink rise up, come after her.

The faucet, moron, I scold myself. I reach for the tap, turning the hot and cold on full-force. The running water blankets the flames that have only just started to grow. The orange danger disappears, but the smoke turns even blacker in the moment of extinction, the smell far more putrid. Like burning flesh. Like what's in that sink isn't wood, but honest-to-God mermaids. Real bodies.

"They'll kill us! Get away, get away!" Mom screams. And even though I know she's got the world muddled, that nothing she does should hurt me because she's not even in the same world I'm in anymore, I look at those mermaids piled in the sink—the ones she's tried to destroy—and I hear her words to the shopkeeper who carved them: *We're just alike, me and Aura.* Suddenly, my heart is in that sink, blackened into some unrecognizable, useless brick of ash.

"Stop," I tell her. "Just stop." I grab her the way Janny sometimes grabs Ethan, scooping him into her arms to keep him from crawling right off the edge of her front porch.

But Mom's still striking the damn matches. And I'm so angry at her—even as my heart is breaking, my anger gains speed. I'm in a car that left *furious* behind a hundred miles ago. I hit the box of matches, knocking them to the ground. They scatter like Mom's thoughts, rolling off in a hundred different directions. She falls to her knees, starts picking the sticks up off the tile, but I stop her. Wrap my arms around her, tightening my grip as she thrashes against me.

I want my arms to be as strong and overpowering as a straitjacket, but Mom breaks away from me, scampering across the linoleum and picking up a match. She tries to strike it, but the head splinters off. "Go," she says, grabbing another match. "A fire. Only way out." Just like she did back at the art museum. "Burn, burny burning," she shouts.

As our fingers tangle in our struggle, Mom starts crying, just like Ethan did that night in the grocery store. Hurt crying. Sick crying. And I know I have to be smart about this. I can't just rope her, this wild thing that'll buck me, knock me to the ground and trample me. I have to pretend; I have to play this game.

"Mom," I say. "Come on—you can't kill a mermaid with fire."

"You can too—"

"Think about it. They're *wet*, Mom. Right? You can't catch something on fire that spends its whole life in the ocean. They're soaked straight to the bone."

"What do I do?" she asks, her eyes as wide as wading pools.

"Suffocate them," I whisper. "Come on."

I motion for her to follow me into the hall. I pull a blanket from the linen closet, then tiptoe back through the living room, toward the kitchen, pretending I don't want the mermaids to hear me sneaking up on them.

Mom screams like some woman being attacked by a serial killer the minute our feet hit the linoleum. She scampers up one of the knocked-over chairs, nearly falling because she doesn't bother to turn it right side up. She makes it onto the table, grabbing all the mermaids above her and yanking them off their fishing line hangers.

"Hurry!" she screams. "Catch them! Catch!"

I drop the blanket to the floor, and start piling the mermaids on top, wondering for a moment how Mom sees this. I try to put on a good show, acting like they're hard to catch, like the mermaids are all flopping like fish in the bottom of a boat. Like their tails are slippery in my hands. Like they're trying to squirm away from me.

When Mom tosses the last of the mermaids down, I gather up the edges of the blanket, making a pouch.

"Oh, God—hurry!" Mom screams. "Watch—watch—"

I stand up, cradling the blanket, and head for the garage. "I'll put them in the trunk, Mom," I ramble, searching for words that might make sense to her. "I'll put them there—with no water—they'll die there. They'll suffocate."

But even as I'm running, it's like the whole world has turned to freaking quicksand.

And Mom's still screaming, Mom's still screaming.

18

~

As van Gogh's talent began to manifest itself, so, tragically, did his declining mental state. Poor Vincent. The classic example of how art takes a person's mind and turns it into cream of chicken soup.

The slam of the Tempo's trunk kills Mom's terrorized wail. She stands in the doorway to the garage, the screen door making her face look gray and hazy.

"We did it, Mom," I say, but when I open that screen, her face doesn't look any brighter.

"It didn't work, Aura," she mumbles as I steer her back through the kitchen, away from the broken threads of fishing line and into the quiet of her bedroom. "I thought it would work, but it didn't. I was so sure, and now, I'm just so tired." Her voice is low and thick. If her voice could be a color, it would be deep midnight blue. A blue so dark, it looks black until you get something else—a sock or a sweater—next to it to compare the shades.

"The mermaids? They're gone, Mom. I suffocated them. You watched me, right?" I push the sketchbooks and canvases off her bed.

"The room, Aura," she says as she crawls across her comforter. "Don't you know anything? The tilty floor that tilted. It didn't work. I had to cover it up."

"It's all right, Mom," I try to soothe her, petting her head. "It's just fine. It's you and me in this together, remember? Just you and me, and we'll work it out." To prove my point, I stay with her on her bed, working her hair loose from its knot. *See, Mom? See? It's okay I can make everything all right and smooth and I will even brush your hair and rub in some leave-in conditioner so it smells like apples like a clean schoolroom when you were whole you were you before all this and it was fine.*

I clean up the bathroom, tossing out the mat, picking up the matches, dousing the whole house with air freshener. When I'm finally done, I check on Mom. I'd hoped she'd sleep it off, you know? Sleep and then wake up and maybe even think that the whole episode with the mermaids had been like some screwed-up dream. A bad nightmare, something she could just wake up from, sweat-soaked, moaning, "Glad *that's* over." But I really should know better by now.

No, after the mermaids, Mom becomes a curlicue. A real curlicue in the middle of her bed. She reminds me of those twirling ribbons I used to doodle down the margins back when I actually went to school. The blankets are piled at her feet, and she just lies there, as the hours slide past, refusing to even roll over.

I don't sleep at all that night—or even try. Instead, I sit in a chair by Mom's bed and watch her. When dawn breaks, all fuzzy and soft, I'm still there, staring at Mom's shoulder blades.

October 27, I scrawl late in the day, in one of the journals Dad gave me. *Mom hasn't spoken in more than twenty-four hours.*

I pour some Gatorade in a glass and drop a straw into it. "Mom," I say, raising her head from the pillow. "Mom, please."

She takes some—but two sips don't seem like enough. I want more—I want to *make* her do more. I want to put a turkey dinner, with dressing and green bean casserole, the works, into a blender until it's soup, and I want to pour it down her throat. But I can't, I have to play her game, because she'll buck me, like a horse at the rodeo. She'll throw me off, and then I'll never get back on again. She'll lock me out completely.

The whiskey bottles haunt me as I continue to plead with her. Two empties, one half-full, one never opened. *You're so lucky,* I remind myself. *She didn't hurt herself—not yet, anyway. This time you could put out the flames. Lucky. Do you even realize how lucky? Do you know the whole house could be a pile of ash if you hadn't come back? Lucky—one crisis averted. But not so fast, look at her here—so depressed, so sad. You still have a decision to make, you know. What are you going to do, Aura? This isn't something you can slam a lid on and walk away from, like you did with the Pilkingtons' bottles. You can't shrug and say it isn't any of your business. You've got to do something. Anything, Aura. Anything.*

"I'm going to leave this Gatorade here on your nightstand, all right, Mom?" I say. "Right here where you can get to it." Because maybe, I think, after last night, me watching like a hawk, she needs to be alone.

She doesn't answer. Part of me wants to bite her, just to get some sound out of her. *Mom,* I feel like shouting, *where the hell did you go this time?*

"How about a little music, huh?" I ask as I head toward her stacks of records. "Something from the archives."

I toss aside a Simon & Garfunkel and a Joni Mitchell—*too quiet, too soft, there's got to be something in here that will wake the dead, maybe Janis, maybe she will scream Mom right back to life.*

I tear through the records too desperately in my search for *Pearl.* The stack teeters; as I race to keep the tower of vinyl from toppling, my hand brushes the sheet Mom's tacked to the wall. Old rusted nails from one of the coffee cans in the garage are pinning the white sheet in a tangled, wrinkled mess. The fabric's actually so crumpled and twisted it looks like a piece of paper somebody wadded into a ball, then tried to smooth out again.

"Is this—is this what you were talking about? What you covered up?" I croak, but she doesn't answer.

I have to look, the same way a doctor has to look at

the long, bloody, slimy trail of intestines flopping out of a car accident victim, so that he can try to figure out how to go about putting Humpty Dumpty back together again.

I slide my fingers underneath the side of the drawn-tight sheet, and tug. Put my foot against the wall for some leverage. Bite down on my lip and really heave. The material finally starts to rip, pulling free of the nails.

A wounded moan oozes out of my mouth when the sheet falls to the carpet. Mom's painted a mural. A whole mural, top to bottom, with shadows and light. She hasn't just left a hundred and thirteen works half-finished, undone, so that she can start yet another. She's *finished* a project. And now that I'm staring, I can't quit. It sucks me in, steals my breath, and refuses to give it back.

It's van Gogh's *Bedroom in Arles*. And then again, it's not. The pictures no longer want to fall from their hangers. The chair doesn't sink into the back wall. The corners are all at perfect right angles. The floor doesn't tilt at all. Everything is as it should be.

I can see her standing at the front of her classroom, telling her students, "That's not the assignment. Draw what you see, not what you think you see."

And it suddenly becomes so clear—the truth climbs up my arms, slides into my ears, and takes root in my brain. In the midst of her madness, Mom's tried to fix her life by painting exactly what she wishes it could be. Nothing out of focus, nothing off-kilter. Nothing off-balance. Nothing skewed. Perfect perspective. That's what she's put in her mural.

"Balance," I mumble. "You were drawing what you *want* to see."

But in the end, she can't paint a scene that will smooth out all her frightening highs and lows. She can't paint away her madness. Can't paint a scene that will finally make her normal. Whole. A scene that will make her turn back into herself.

That's what she wants, though—that's what she's asking me for. Her mural is a flare in the nighttime sky, a message in a bottle, a scream from the far shore. Mom wants me to help her. Wants me to rescue her.

I'm in the kitchen, suddenly, flipping through the phone book, the yellow pages, *photography,* and there it is: *Zellers*, in a half-page color ad. But before I even reach for the phone, I'm thinking about the time when I was twelve and Mom disappeared. The final-straw episode. The event that brought meds home. The event that, looking back, must have allowed Dad to start scouring the earth for a something-better woman. That led him to Brandi.

I could mark how long Mom had been gone by how many half-eaten ham sandwiches were piled on the kitchen table. How many flies danced over the mayonnaise-laden wheat bread. The flies, they didn't care that Mom was just an empty seat, a faint smell, a person who should be there but wasn't.

No, the flies didn't care, but I did—so much, I hardly had enough room in my body for all my fear. I had terror crammed inside me, shoved as tight as a bulky winter sweater in a vanity drawer meant only for a hairbrush.

Even Dad, who'd already refused to rescue me on the soccer field, he couldn't sleep. Pretended he wasn't smoking again. Each night, he slapped together sandwiches for dinner and we tried to eat them, tried, but wound up only taking a bite out of the top corners and leaving the rest on our plastic plates.

We went through this frantic searching back then, like, say, you can't find a family heirloom—a ring, passed down from your mother and your mother's mother before that. And you're tearing the whole house up, tossing bedspreads back and running your hand along the carpet and draining the fish tank and even taking out all the chuck roasts from the freezer because you got food out of there yesterday—and who knows? It could have slipped off anywhere.

Dad called Mom's old yoga instructor and a friend who'd moved to Wales.

"She took money, Aura," Dad told me. "She could be anywhere. Anywhere in the whole world."

"Maybe we should call Nell," I said, reaching into the dustiest corners of my brain for an answer.

Dad glared at me like I'd suggested maybe we were better off without Mom. And then his face softened out, like he was reminding himself I was only twelve years old, and I really didn't know what I was saying.

"Anywhere in the world but there," Dad said. "Grace would *never* go to Nell's. And don't you dare call her, either, all right? If Nell knows your mother is gone, there's no telling what she'll try to do. Look, I know Grace never said this right out, but—Nell put someone away before, Aura.

Grace's dad. We don't want that, do we? We don't want Mom to go away?"

I shook my head, my face quivering like some little baby's.

"All right," Dad sighed, rubbing the back of his neck. "It's okay—we'll figure it out, just—don't ever call your grandmother, all right? Don't ever call Nell."

We reported it to the police—missing persons. *No, sir, no tattoos, no scars, just long black hair and an even longer, even darker history with schizophrenia.* And still, then, Dad cared enough to want her back. Cared enough not to want her locked away.

It took two days (felt like centuries) for the call to finally come. Mom was in Colorado. It was the first plane ride I ever took.

"She said that she thought if she got up high enough, she could leave it all behind," a police officer told Dad when we rushed in and there she was, in the Denver police station, all wrapped up in a blanket. "She said she thought a mountain would do it."

"*She* said, *she* said," Mom snickered. It had been a shock to see her all hunched over. I'd never seen anyone look so defeated before. Because even then, I think, she knew meds were coming. How could she *not* know, the way the fear in Dad's face had instantly been replaced by *fed up* when they'd looked at each other?

I stare down at the phone book's yellow page entry, remembering how Dad had told me, even as he must have been sketching the blueprints for his escape plan, even as he was deciding he'd had his fill, *Never call your grandmother.*

I slam the phone book shut, dip my head into the fridge, grab the Gatorade. I carry it to Mom's room where I top up her already-full glass, replacing the two measly sips she's taken.

19

~

The Sylvia Plath effect refers to the phenomenon that creative writers are more susceptible to mental illness. Especially females who write poetry. I am such a goner.

October 28, I scrawl in one of Dad's journals. *I fed Mom an orange and some chicken broth.* It's the only highlight of the day.

I pace, I watch, I pet. The clock ticks.

I try to eat. I gag when food hits my tongue.

October 29, I write. *I think if I could just get some sleep, I could wake up with an answer. I'd be able to figure this mess out.* But sleep doesn't come—not for me, not during the day, or even in the dead of night. Sleep plays hide-and-seek with me. I hunt for it, rolling fitfully on the couch, or curling under a blanket in the chair by Mom's bed. I even try to crawl into bed with Mom, taking up Dad's old place, hoping that having another body so close to her—warm and breathing and real—will help her turn toward something solid and true.

But it doesn't. And lying next to Mom doesn't help me catch a single wink, either. Sleep is crafty—it's sneaky—and even as I call its name, it refuses to show its stupid face.

Somewhere close to midnight, after having paced through every room upstairs, I wander down into the basement. The whole place is just as cluttered and scattered as Mom's brain. I hate the junk we've hung onto—a bicycle with no wheels, canvases Mom's gessoed, half-used tubes of oil and acrylic paints, laundry baskets full of dirty clothes, even an open two-liter of flat Coke sitting on the bottom stair. But what's the point of cleaning up? It'd be like shoving a metaphorical Kleenex into the bullet hole that has become my life with Mom.

I kick at the dusty, stray branches of an artificial Christmas tree, finding an old journal beneath the plastic greenery. Little does Dad know, I don't usually fill the pages up with Mom's every waking mood (and the fact that I *have* been taking notes on Mom's condition lately shows just how deep my fear is starting to sink). No, for the most part, I sketch in the journals, and write poetry. Just like a junkie who will get high on anything—even glue.

I plop on the once-loved orange velour couch that's now sprouting stuffing, and open the journal to find Jeremy staring up at me from the first page. Last summer, I'd penciled in his gorgeous face, his beauty mark, the wind blowing his hair across one eye. Looking at the drawing, everything I wish I could tell him explodes through me. And even though it's honestly the last thing I want to do, I'm scrawling a poem right over his cheek...

The skies cloud over,
the smell of thunder taints the air,
and the rain begins to fall
from my eyes.

There's a book of poetry
in the lines of my hands
that no one wants to read.

I've lived my life
rooted in her darkness,
arms catatonic as a tree,
unable to run or cry
when her Other prunes my flowers.

And my book of poetry
has been erased
before anyone could read it.

Morning, October 30, I scrawl in my journal. *Mom still hasn't spoken. I keep putting Neosporin on her feet where the matches hit her, and even though the burns look sore, she doesn't flinch. I gave her a sponge bath, and I realized she'd gotten her period.*

I finally got the bloody sheet out from under her, and rolled her onto a clean one. I've never had to change Mom's pads before, and it scares me. It scares me so much. Yesterday, I could only get her to drink some fluids. How long can a person go without solid food???

I sigh and look over my shoulder at Mom's mural. Everything is so bad. Everything seems so wrong, so wrong, and my stupid words in a journal that nobody reads—what good are they? But I have nobody on my side, *nobody*, and my pen is moving again, because writing is all I have left…

She painted a poem
on a wall
so the world would understand
and love her.
But not one set of yellow eyes
wandered for a second.
Now her poem stands
unnoticed and neglected.
And I think that she should
never paint again.

I sang a song
to my best friend
so that she could understand
and love me.
But my melody sent her away.
And now I stand
friendless and rejected.

And I think that I should
never sing again.

I wrote a poem
and gave it to my mother.
I filled it with visions
and voices as beautiful as she.
But it left her bruised,
beaten with its awful truths.
Now I stand
motherless and detached.
And I think that I should never write again.

I'm already running for the kitchen trash can as I crumple up the page. But this whole situation is so screwed up, once I've tossed my poem in with the old soggy coffee grounds and yesterday's newspaper, I need a crutch more than I ever have before. So I snatch up my last cigarette and the box of matches I hid behind the only cereal box in the cabinet. As I light the cigarette and take what should be the first sweet drag, I think about the mermaids. My ears ring with the echo of that awful smoke detector. And the smoke that fills my mouth doesn't taste comforting at all—it tastes like fury, like illness.

Like poetry.

Suddenly, I'm back at the trash can, fishing out my poem. I'm tossing it into the bowl and lighting the edges of the paper with my cigarette. Because it's not enough just to throw it away. I've got to obliterate it. I don't want my poem to exist *anywhere* in the world—even a landfill. Watching the flame engulf the page, I get it—Mom's need to destroy those mermaids. Sick as it was, I understand.

But once my poem turns to a wad of black char, I don't feel satisfied. It's not enough.

I suddenly know for certain I've got to get rid of it, this thing, this *art addiction* that's holding the two of us down. They—all the experts—*THEY* say a drunk is always a drunk because the desire never goes away. But if boozers like the Pilkingtons would just stay *away* from the sauce, then *voilà!* No more blackouts, no more projectile vomiting, no more delirium tremens, right? So if I got rid of the art, all the supplies, if I took away our ability to get wasted on our own imagination, our own creativity, couldn't I cure us both? Especially Mom?

I mean, they're the same, right? Creative and crazy. And it won't be easy, because it's the one thing Mom and I love more than any other, that makes us whole—but isn't that how a druggie feels about her needles? Doesn't she think it's the thing that makes her complete? The thing that allows her to function? And if all those people in A.A. and N.A. can walk away from the bottle, the pills, the powder, then Mom and I could walk away, too, right? Mom could tie her hair up on her head and get some job doing *taxes,* right? And never look back, and be the most straight-and-narrow gal on the block?

I race down the hallway. In my bedroom, I grab up all my new journals, every single stupid one. *But these are still blank,* I remind myself. So I'm racing to the basement, little whelps escaping my lips like I'm running from a maniac in a ski mask who's just broken into the house. I kick, I throw, I dig through the remnants of a life that had only *seemed* happy, once, to a little girl who didn't completely understand everything that was really happening. I pluck the journals from the floor, the old couch, the stairs. These books seethe with drawings and poetry—some completed, some only shards. Pages and pages of danger, carcinogens, poison.

Pages tossed at me by a dad I can't turn to. Pages—that's all I have. Goddamned empty *pages.* Because people leave. And here I am, a dark hole that everyone avoids—*Watch out, you don't want to fall, you don't want to end up down there. You just may never get out again...*

I'm so worked up, I don't even have a heart anymore, but a hot, pulsing fist of rage. I'm practically growling as I rush outside to the burn pile in the center of our yard—the chicken wire circle where I'd piled all Mom's torn-up rose bushes. (Joey was right, the garbage man really won't take yard waste. Besides, after finding those damned whiskey bottles, trash cans had become way too heavy, too serious. Wasn't it enough that I had to bear my own family's darkest truths?)

I toss my journals on top, then race back inside. Dart down the hall, into Mom's room, where I start to gather up all of the half-finished canvases she's tossed behind her shoulder, like a superstitious person tossing salt to avoid bad luck.

"I'm doing what you wanted, Mom," I tell her as I tuck

a canvas under my arm. "I'm finishing it, okay? I think—maybe I just shouldn't have stopped you. Maybe, if I'd let you burn those stupid mermaids, maybe you wouldn't be here like this now. So—breathe deep, Mom. Because I'm doing it for you, okay? I'm getting rid of all of it, right? I'm taking care of it," I swear, desperation making my voice sound electric.

I'm all Hunchback of Notre Dame as I'm trying to keep from dropping the canvases. I pause in the middle of the kitchen to stare at the skateboard in the back corner. I know I should grab it, too—it's the same as any canvas, the way I've been aching to paint it—but it's not mine to destroy, really, so I dart past it, lugging only Mom's artwork out to the burn pile.

Back inside, I snatch up the morning's newspaper. I'm still frantically twisting pages into ropes as I seize the remaining matches from the counter. I push the glass door open, expecting the mermaids to start thunking against each other, just like they always do. It's like a fall down a dark mineshaft, remembering that the mermaids aren't on the ceiling anymore.

I light match after match, just like Mom—God, dare I think it? *Just like Mom.* Only not—I'm not hallucinating. I don't think mermaids are trying to kill me. I know what's what. This isn't an act *of* crazy, it's an act to get *rid* of it. *Right?*

"Come on," I snarl, igniting the paper ropes. "Come *on.*" The bushes have all dried, become kindling. Flames spread faster than disease. Soon, the entire bin is engulfed.

Paint chemicals fuel the blaze, causing the flames to swallow each other, explode. The tower of heat grows and multiplies, gains strength, until it isn't a tower at all. Isn't something stationary, something cemented into one spot. It's a cyclone, spinning, twirling, threatening to break out from the pitiful chicken wire that encircles it.

I keep the fire inside the bin by wetting the grass around it with the hose. I aim the nozzle at a nearby tree anytime the flames get the bright idea of licking the autumn-dry branches. Eventually, the blaze starts to die, but my emotions don't. I've got millions of fire ants under my skin, eating me from the inside-out. Actually, once the backyard inferno is reduced to a smoking pile of ash, I feel even more desperate. Woman-at-the-scene-of-a-natural-disaster desperate. The earth has folded in on top of me.

I need to try something. God. Anything. No *way* am I going to torch Mom's old paintings, those she finished before she frayed like a shoelace (they're just too beautiful—it'd break my heart), but I'm suddenly racing back into the house and into Mom's room. It reeks of paint fumes—probably from her fresh mural—and my body heaves with tears, because I know, with absolute certainty, not a shred of doubt about it, that it's also the smell of her madness.

The mural is the painting I'd really like to incinerate. But it's not as if I can tear the wall off like the top sheet of a sketchbook, crumple it, and toss it into the burn bin. So

I rip the lid off a can of white, and pour it sloppily into a tray. I grab a matted roller, dunk it in. Paint dripping, I carry the roller to the wall where I start to paint right over Mom's *Bedroom in Arles.* Where I erase it, like I want to erase her madness. Paint right over it, like a scab over a wound.

"*Look,*" I say when I'm done. I race to the bed, try to prop Mom's head up. But her eyes roll in her head like olives on a plate.

I pace her room nervously, drop the needle on the record that's still on her turntable, and finally head into the kitchen to make Mom a V8 with a straw. As I'm coming back down the hall, I'm hoping, like an idiot, that the music will have perked Mom up a little. But when I get to her room, she's still in the same position I left her, curlicue that she is.

I crawl onto her bed. "Mom, here, this will make you feel better. Mom? Mom?" I put the straw in her mouth, but her lips don't tighten around it.

"Please, Mom," I say. "You've got to drink. If you won't eat, you've got to drink." I put the straw in her mouth again, but she won't take it. It's like I'm putting a straw through the mouth hole of a rubber Halloween mask.

And of all things, I realize that the record on Mom's turntable is still that damned Pink Floyd—the same album that was playing the day I came home from school to find Mom working, insisting she wasn't broken, wasn't sick. A day when I still had time, when I could think Mom only *seemed* as far as another universe… now, she *is* gone. She's in another dimension. Like a comatose patient. Like the fucking dead.

A lonely acoustic guitar fills the room as "Wish You Were Here" begins to ooze through the speakers. But it's just too close to how I feel—I'm so exposed; my skin isn't just raw, but turned inside-out. I slam the V8 onto the nightstand and race to Mom's record player. I throw the arm to the side, dragging the needle across the vinyl with a screech that sounds like an angry cat.

"*Enough!*" I shriek. I cry and wail like I'm really all alone, like there's no one in the room to even hear me. Because there isn't. There's just me and this corpse who used to be someone I recognized.

Yeah, a corpse. Standing on the word makes me seasick, at first. But then, instead of making me feel rotten, it gives me an idea. Maybe not a great idea, but I'm grasping at the broken-off remnants of straws here.

"Okay, Mom," I say, pulling the crystals from her drawer and arranging them in a semi-circle around her bed. "You know what we're going to do?" I ask her. "We're going to have a séance. That's exactly right. Just like in all your new-age, metaphysics books, right? Like the time we tried to contact your father all those years ago. Remember that? You, me, and Dad calling out to your father. And maybe it didn't work then, Mom, maybe you didn't get to talk to him, but it *will* work this time—I promise. I won't giggle and screw it all up like I did when I was little. A séance. We're going to pull you back, Mom. We're going to get you out of no-man's land. We're bringing you straight back into the land of the living. Do you hear me, Mom? Just believe in it, okay? Believe in me, and these crystals. These powerful, healing, vibrating crystals. These crystals *work*, okay? You were right all along. Believe in every single word I'm telling you, because I'm going to pull you back."

There's no one else's hand to hold, so I just take Mom's hands. Mom's pale, limp fingers.

"Oh, great powers that be," I say. "Oh, otherworld, oh—give us the power," I say, my voice shaking like a bowl of Jell-O because I don't know what I'm doing, I'm winging it, and it all feels like bull. "Give us the power to return Grace Ambrose. Grace Ambrose, born April 3, 1970. Grace Ambrose, lover of peanut butter and bacon sandwiches, art, and Aura—lover—" My voice quivers— "of Aura Ambrose. We beg of you, please allow her safe return. She *belongs* in the real world. Her name is Grace Ambrose, and she's *not dead yet.*"

But just looking at her, you'd never know that was actually true. The tears that have made silver stripes down my cheeks start dripping right off the edge of my jaw. And I can't even talk anymore.

20

~

When you are caring for a schizo,
it is vitally important not to neglect
the other relationships in your family.

Half an hour later, I'm standing on the sidewalk in front of Zellers Photography. I stare through the front window until Nell steps into view. Comes into the front room to answer the phone. Says a few words into the receiver and shuffles some papers on a desk. Looks up for just a second, and gives me a double take. Says something else into her phone—maybe, "Let me call you back"?

I'm shaking. I want to run, but I can't; my feet are like gnarly tree roots that have worked their way through the sidewalk. I've torn up all the gray concrete, just like a tree that tears a headstone in two in an ancient cemetery. I've ruined everything, no surprise there—Aura Ambrose, World's Biggest Fuck-Up. Can't even take care of my mother, can't help her, what a joke I am. What a pathetic excuse. I'm nothing special. Nothing, nothing special.

Nell opens the front door of her photography studio and glares at me.

I try to open my mouth, but nothing comes out. I'm dirty, because who can bother with shampoo at a time like this? And I'm wearing the same unwashed hoodie I've had on for three days, and I wonder—who wants to be the grandmother of a girl like me? But I don't exactly have many choices here, in the corner I've backed myself into. I ache to tell this woman standing in front of me that we're like rungs on a ladder with only one step between us. I try to form the word—*grandmother*—but all that comes out is a pitiful, "Guh—"

I wish I *had* been transparent during those weekends I'd spent with Nell, working not so much out of a need for pocket money as a need to see her, to know what her voice sounds like. I wish she'd known all along that I'd wanted to get close to something that Dad had snatched away—*family.* Wanted to know, again, what that gorgeous nest of a word really *felt* like.

This is a bad idea, I tell myself. *A really bad idea*... How can I explain all this? And why would Nell *want* to help? No one else does. Nobody—not Dad, or Janny.

And besides, *Never contact your grandmother. She put*

someone away once. I turn on my heel and start to head back for the Tempo.

"*Aura*," Nell calls. And the sound of my own name—it's like electricity, you know? Like I'm standing there on a downed power line.

When I turn, we stare at each other a minute, three squares of sidewalk and sixteen years between us. *A lifetime ago, I could've been a granddaughter. Today, I'm a nuisance.*

But Nell, her eyes get wide and fearful behind those enormous glasses. Like she knows. *Does she?* "How's—your mom—how's—Grace?" she finally asks.

I'm just so desperate—my face is wrinkling and I stink—I *stink*—and I can't take it anymore, so I'm crying and everything is wrong and I thought I could fix it but I can't I can't I can't.

"I think—I think she might be dying," I say.

21

~

Catatonia can include stupor or bizarre posturing, as well as either extreme rigidity or flexibility of the limbs. See also: Inanimate Object.

Nell flips the *Closed* sign to face the street, and before I know it, like she's some kind of pickpocket or something, she's got the keys to the Tempo. She speeds through the streets like she's a cop on a prime-time detective show. I sit in the passenger's seat like some half-assed, hopeless sidekick Nell doesn't trust to drive.

And suddenly, we're home, inside, though I don't remember coming up the front walk. I'm showing Nell the way down the hall, and she's following so close behind me that she steps all over my heels.

"Grace," Nell says as soon as she explodes into the bedroom. "Grace," she tries again, rustling Mom's shoulder. She pushes Mom's hair out of the way—the same hair I worked loose of its knot and brushed soft. She leans down so that her lips are about a millimeter away from Mom's ear. "*Grace!*" she screams.

But Mom doesn't move. It's like Nell's just whispered in her ear.

"How long has she been like this?" she asks me.

"I—I don't." I can't even remember, everything's so jumbled. When did she finish her mural? Two days ago? A day and a half? Three?

Stupidly, I twirl around, looking for the journal I'd desperately started to scrawl notes in as Mom started to deteriorate—the same journal I've already reduced to ash. It's like I'm suddenly on fire and I can't remember what I'm supposed to do. Sit, stop—no—stop, drop, and—and *what?*

Nell grabs the phone and dials 9-1-1. "Schizophrenic," she says. "Catatonic."

The paramedics show up—but they just look so wrong. It's so *wrong* that they're rolling that stretcher over Mom's scattered, balled-up drop cloths and pulling up her eyelids and thumping around on her.

"Just a few days," I hear myself telling them. "Before, she was working day and night—she's a painter."

"Manic, was she?" one of them asks.

Manic? Is that right? I nod. I think so.

"She was eating day before yesterday—a little. Yesterday, just fluids. Gatorade and V8. But today—I can't get anything down her." And then a thought occurs to me that scares me so much, tears come, instant and effortless. "It hasn't already been too long, has it?" I ask the paramedics. "It hasn't been too long without food?"

"We're going to do everything we can," the medics say, and before I can get my bearings, we're all rushing out the front door, and the red and blue lights are swirling, and the neighbors have all come out to watch—even the damned Pilkingtons—and *this is wrong, all wrong, Mom will never forgive me*, but I let myself be swept inside the ambulance. Swept, like a piece of dust onto a dustpan.

Let me tell you something—the inside of an ambulance is one thing you never want to see for yourself. It means that the whole world has just gone to shit.

It means that death is dancing at your door.

22

~

Hospitalization usually occurs during or after a psychotic episode.

Dad comes. I guess wonders never cease. He actually comes to the emergency room. But he doesn't come to me. I'm sitting in a chair right by the door, tear-streaked face, hugging my knees to my chest, and he heads straight for Nell. I feel like a piece of freaking trash that no one wants to bother with or be around. Everyone probably thinks I've really screwed the whole thing up. And the sad truth is, I have. Look where we are.

They're talking, and Dad is pointing at Nell—*you, you*—making air-jabs at her chest. And she's jabbing back—

no, you; no, you. Blame like a game of hot potato. Every once in a while, Dad glances over at me, but since I'm just this smelly hunk of his former life, he doesn't even attempt to ask me if I'm okay.

I tune them out and stare at Dad's sweater—this time it's black, probably cashmere—and the pink striped shirt collar folded down neatly over the sweater's neckband.

I picture Brandi buying that pink shirt at the same ritzy men's clothing store where she buys all Dad's clothes. Imagine her charging it on one of her 153 credit cards, and bringing it home to the loft. I can see Dad gushing over it, too—the man who used to say that Christmas shouldn't bring a single store-bought gift. I'll bet he practically slobbered all over that designer shirt that Brandi bought him, not even for Christmas or a birthday, but *just because*, and it probably cost more than groceries for his family for the week.

Now that Dad and Nell are through pointing and jabbing, their heads are bobbing—*yes, yes, yes.*

"I agree," I hear Dad say. "One of my greatest regrets is that we didn't do that years ago."

I know what they're talking about I may be a lot of things, but I'm no dope. And I feel like shit because, after these years of being in it together, I've done the unthinkable, the unforgivable. I've given her up. I've handed her off to the enemy.

They're going to send her away. And it's a selfish thought, I know it is, but I wonder—*What will happen to* me *now?*

I'm at the freaking breaking point. So I bolt—right out of my chair and the waiting room and the hospital itself.

But, come on, where did I think I was going? The Tempo's still at home since I came to the hospital in the ambulance. And it's way too dark now to even consider hoofing it. Pitch black sky and glittering stars above, à la *Starry Night.*

I hate, hate, *hate* that picture.

So I plop down on the sidewalk. And when I put my hands in my lap, I hear an old pack of cigarettes I'd forgotten about crinkle in the front pocket of my hoodie. I light up right there, even though the cigarettes are maybe six months old, stale as molded bread, and even though there's probably some ordinance against smoking so close to the hospital.

In front of me, the parking lot lights pop to life. A helicopter swarms overhead—probably some car accident victim, I think. What I wouldn't give to trade places with them, because anything would be better than knowing that I put my mother away, that I sent her to a fate worse than death. I've tied a box of TNT to all the promises I made—no pills, no doctors, no Dad, no Nell.

Boom.

Footsteps clicking on the sidewalk get me geared up for a fight. *Just try it. You just try to take this cigarette and I will scratch your eyes out. I am so ready to kick somebody's ass. I dare you. Tell me—*

But whoever it is doesn't say anything—just sits down beside me on the sidewalk.

When I turn, there she is, white hair and black glasses.

"This sure is some shitty coffee," Nell says, pointing at the cup she's gotten from the hospital vending machine. "But you can have some if you want."

"No, thanks," I say, hiding my cigarette and knocking it out against the sidewalk, because Nell would probably put me away for cigarettes, for all I know.

"No, no, don't mind me," Nell says. "You go on. I respect a girl who doesn't let some arbitrary rule like 'must be eighteen to purchase' get in her way."

I shrug and pull another cigarette out of my dwindling pack. And because she's being cool about this, at least, I light one for her, too.

"Wow," she says. "March 15, 1982—last time I had one of those." She shakes her head and gives me this *please, don't* look, like I'm some sort of drug pusher, *Come on, Nell. Don't be lame. Everybody's doing it.* "What the hell," she finally says, and slips it from my fingers.

"You know," Nell says after a cloudy exhale, "I thought I had it all figured out when I was young. *Freedom*. God. I didn't need anybody's rules. Nobody gonna tell me what I could and couldn't do. Nobody gonna tell me I had to get married—so what if I was pregnant? What did that mean? I got married on my *own* terms. Because of love, not biology. Grace was four," she adds quietly, like a side note. "She was my flower girl." Her eyes get this funny, faraway, inward look, until she shakes her head and brings her thoughts back on track.

"And so what if I used to like to smoke every once in

a while?" she asks. "What if," Nell confesses, leaning in to whisper in my ear, "what if, even, I liked a little weed? Really," she goes on, her voice gathering strength, "so *what*? I mean, so what if I decide to drink my lunch? So what if I eat a whole chocolate cake for dinner, nothing else? Who am I hurting other than me, right?"

I nod, watching as she takes another drag on her cigarette. After a few minutes, she takes off her glasses. Her eyes are all watery and her nose is turning red, even though it's really not all that cold outside tonight. "Only maybe I *did* hurt somebody else," she says. "Maybe the way I lived, maybe it was wrong. Maybe I did something…"

We sit there a few more minutes, just sit and smoke.

"She said we were in it together," I finally tell Nell. "She depended on me, you know? Because she didn't want to be medicated anymore, like Dad made her. Because she—"

"God, we used to fight," Nell interrupts. "I never fought with anyone the way I fought with her. Not even my own parents. I slapped her one time—not *one* slap, but once, when I was mad, I started slapping her until her cheeks were bright red. *Flaming.* Because I knew it—she hadn't been diagnosed yet, but I knew there was something about her—it wasn't just adolescent bullshit. And she blamed me, you know, for the way her dad died. Blamed me—we were in the midst of this awful tug of war. Her wanting me to tell her I'd done something wrong, that I'd made a mistake with her dad. Me wanting to make her *less* like him. Because we knew, both of us, what was happening. I knew. And she must've thought I was being so cruel that day when I started slapping her, but I was so scared, so desperate, and it was like I thought I could beat it out of her.

"Beat it," she repeats, shaking her head, spitting a chuckle like it's the most harebrained thing she's ever heard, even to this day. "Like dust out of a rug."

She takes another drag and shakes her head. I remember how angry I was at Mom for clipping the strings in the Ambrose Original, and I know exactly how easy it would be to lash out in frustration.

"I don't think I was supposed to be somebody's mother. I'm just—toxic." Nell shudders.

I light another cigarette for myself and hand another to Nell, too. Because we're laying it all out on the line, I say, "I guess at least I know what to expect when I go nuts."

"Oh, please," Nell says. "You're not going nuts."

I'm offended at how easily she can dismiss this, brush it away like it's a gnat. "Everybody in my family goes nuts."

"Thanks a lot," Nell says.

"You know what I mean. Come on—my mom *and* my grandfather. You can't deny that it runs in the family."

"Yeah, well, so does heart trouble," Nell says, snatching the cigarette out of my hand. She drops it to the pavement and snuffs it out with her shoe. But she keeps hers burning.

"Oh, Aura," she sighs after our quiet grows cumbersome. "You're the sanest person I know. Ever since you first set foot in my studio—I knew exactly who you were. God, you look so much like your mom did at your age. You're almost her exact double. Except for the eyes. I've seen madness up close, twice, you know," she says softly. "It doesn't have you."

Quiet settles between us. I'm not sure how Nell can make such a damned sweeping statement. It almost seems like a stereotype. *All women are bad drivers. All black people can dance. All granddaughters are safe from mental illness.*

"I admire you," she says. "I really do. You should be proud of yourself, truly. You took good care of her."

"Big deal."

"It *is* a big deal. You took far better care of her than I did, and I'm her mother. You did it, Aura. You did good, hon. Real good."

"What good did it do *her*?" I scream. *Oh, here we go, now I'm exploding.* "Big deal, Nell. I took care of her. For *what*? So you can put her away? I *know* you're going to put her away."

"What were you going to do, Aura? Were you just going to sit in that house with her the rest of your life? You'll be graduating before you know it. Were you going to give up on college? Or were you going to take her with you? Set up your mentally ill mother in your dorm room?"

Bull's-eye for Nell, but there's no way I'm going to tell her she's right. "You can't just lock her away like you did her dad!" I scream. "She's Grace Ambrose, born April 3, 1970. She is your daughter, and *she is still alive.*"

"Whoa—" Nell says, holding her hand up. Her cigarette has burned all the way down to the filter but she hasn't noticed, and when it starts to singe her fingers, she just drops it onto the parking lot, lets it roll away. She keeps her eyes on me the whole time.

I'd almost forgotten what it was like to have somebody look at me. Really look, and see me.

"I'm not shutting her away, locking her up, no key. I'm not *institutionalizing* her, Aura."

"You're not?" I say. I'm blubbering, just like a little kid, like some baby.

"No—honey. No. A short-term care facility."

"Short-term," I repeat. "She's coming back?"

"Yes—yes."

I stare at her, mouth dangling open. *How is this possible? How can this be? She comes back? She comes* back?

"How have you been managing to juggle school and your mother?"

I shrug.

"Well, that's the first thing that's going to change," Nell says. "I'm going with you to that school of yours tomorrow, and I'm fixing everything. Get you right back on track, you hear me?"

I tug my sweatshirt over my hands, like Katie Pretti in English class.

"And after we're done there, you can help me move my elliptical trainer."

"Move your—what?" My brain is spinning.

"My trainer. I can't go a day without it. I've got a bird, too. You like birds? Nasty creatures, birds. Worse than men, sometimes. 'Course, if I get too sick of the bird, I can always roast it."

I keep staring at her, bewildered.

"Look, I'm not going to leave you alone while your mother's gone. I know I haven't been any kind of a grandmother to you, but I think it's high time I started, all right?"

"High time—"

"I don't snore, I make a mean veal parmesan, and I even promise not to make fun of your mother's decorating."

"So you're moving in," I say slowly, though it doesn't seem real.

"Temporarily. Unless, of course, you'd rather stay with your father." She wrinkles her nose with disgust.

"Mom'll never go for this," I say.

"Oh, yes, she will. She's not exactly capable of arguing right now, anyway. And when she *is*—" Nell shakes her head. "I may have been out of the picture awhile, but I've known her a very long time, Aura. I'm going to make her see things my way. This time, I'm not going to slink away."

I stare into Nell's cloudless blue eyes, not wanting to scream for the first time in what feels like forever. *Is it possible?* I start to wonder. *Do things really work out in the end?* I get the weird feeling that maybe, even in the midst of a psychotic break, Mom was right about something. Maybe we *do* pedal the earth with our feet—and maybe, just maybe, mine have made the whole world start to turn around.

23

~

Many family members of the clinically cuckoo say they wish they'd known that feelings of shame and guilt were normal.

"I'm very disappointed in your behavior as of late, Aura," Fritz says as soon as Nell and I step into her office that looks, this morning, like the inside of a cheerleader's bedroom after a slumber party: pom-poms all over the floor, red and white cheering sneakers on top of her filing cabinet, and about fifty soda cans strewn all over her desk and the chairs. The only difference between this scene and a real cheerleader's bedroom is that the cans don't say *diet* all down the sides. A giant banner stretched across the length of her office screams *CONGRATS CRESTVIEW!*

FIRST PLACE IN SQUAD SHOWDOWN 8 YRS. IN A ROW!

At least someone had an oh-so happy-dappy weekend.

"Ve-wy disappointed, Auwa," Fritz says, this time around an extra large bite of her breakfast biscuit. She balls up the McDonald's wrapper and tosses it toward the trash can for a three-pointer. She misses.

She slurps the last watery drops out of an enormous plastic cup—the kind you can pick up at any Kum & Go—and instantly, I'm thinking about home. Because there are about a hundred of those cups in my kitchen cabinets. I guess some people really do have matching juice glass sets, but Mom and I are more like gas station plastic freebies we rinse out and reuse.

God, I miss her.

"Sorry," Fritz says to Nell, once she finally swallows her enormous ball of McCud. "Just finishing up breakfast." She grabs her second Big Gulp of Dr Pepper and starts sucking away at the straw to wash it all down. Glares at me so hard that I swear I can actually see the grease from her last three Egg McMuffins (the wrappers are all balled up on her desk) slide right into her frown wrinkles.

As any of the cheerleaders that Mrs. Fritz sponsors would say, *Ick.*

"Leaving campus again with no permission," Fritz chastises. "Taking a non-excused extended absence."

I'm already uncomfortable, because Nell has insisted that I not wear my jeans, like I wanted. She's given me a pair of green plaid slacks and an enormous red jasper necklace, declaring all the while that green and red are, in fact, complimentary colors and go perfectly well together (*What's the matter with you? You should know this. Didn't your mother the painter teach you anything at all?),* and telling me that I should never approach any kind of superior looking like a little piece of fluff.

"Fluff gets flicked off of the lapel of a suit jacket," Nell told me. "Don't get flicked away, Aura."

I catch my reflection in the glass panel in Fritz's door, surprised again at how nicely my hips fill out Nell's pants. And I actually like the way her blouse fits my cantaloupe-sized boobs. It crosses my mind that maybe I really wouldn't mind tossing all my oversized hoodies, but I still feel a little silly in the getup. Like I'm a little miniature Nell—all I need to do is bleach my hair stark white and we'd be twins.

And here Fritz is, glaring at me like the fluff Nell warned me not to be. I want to say, *See? I could have worn my silly old jeans for this shit,* but I don't. I slump down into a chair and think, *Great. Here we go, here we go...*

"Excuse me?" Nell snaps. "You're disappointed in *her*?"

Her tone makes me slide right back up, a smile slowly spreading across my cheeks. *Well, well, well. What do we have here...*

"Do you have any idea what this girl has been through in the past few weeks?" Nell asks. "Have you any idea what she's been through these past sixteen *years*?"

Fritz gulps. "Ms.—Ms. Ambrose."

"Zellers," Nell corrects. "Aura's grandmother."

"School policy dictates that I deal only with a guardian or parent—"

"I *am* the guardian," Nell says.

"But why—where—why—" Fritz stammers.

"Because her mother has been committed to a short-term care facility."

"Committed?"

Nell nods. "For schizophrenia."

"For—*what*?" Fritz asks, picking up a heap of manila folders to expose an entire Pizza Hut box. "What? What?"

"Don't tell me you weren't aware of her mother's condition," Nell snaps. "She was diagnosed back in 1988."

"No—this sort of thing—not as though Aura has the condition herself—our concern—not parental afflictions—" Fritz blubbers.

"It should be in her permanent record, shouldn't it?" Nell asks.

Fritz scrambles to her feet and rushes to a beat-up metal filing cabinet. She opens a drawer (which I half expect to be full of crushed KFC buckets) and pulls out a file. She carries it to her desk, her pantyhose-packed thighs zipping against the material of her businesswoman skirt, and opens it up. "No—see here? On the first day of school, when asked to fill out her in-case-of-emergency card, Aura didn't indicate—"

Nell shoots me a glare. I shrug. Why would I think it was any of their business? Why would I want the faculty's busybody noses stuck so far up in my face, I could see the black hairs poking out their nostrils?

"Aura has actually been her mother's primary caregiver since her parents' divorce three years ago," Nell sighs. "I regret that I wasn't there to help, I'll admit that. But I'm here now. And at least *I* was there when Aura reached out. It's my understanding that Aura was in this very office talking to *you* when her mother's condition was deteriorating. You have a very bright student in your office—a student who is suddenly cutting class—"

"Yes, but Aura began to make it something of a habit, leaving school grounds. On several different occasions—"

"My *dear* woman," Nell says (and I love that she's tossed such a condescending *dear* at Fritz, I love it, I love it), "it seems to me that you had ample opportunity to find out what was going on in Aura's home. Why was there no attempt to contact Mr. Ambrose? Hmm? A call from your office surely would have alerted Aura's father that there was a problem. Perhaps, if you had placed that simple phone call, Aura's mother would not have reached the point of needing hospitalization."

Fritz just gulps and—*I wish I had a camera*—folds her hands over her desktop and nods.

"I believe that it's high time you started digging a little deeper to find out what's going on with some of your students," Nell says. "It shouldn't be that much work; you only have to deal with last names beginning with A, B, or C—and eat all day, apparently."

Fritz flinches.

"I want an office runner sent right this minute to collect the assignments Aura's missed the past few days. She will start back to class full time tomorrow morning. With," she adds, tossing a look my way, "a good portion if not the vast majority of her assignments completed."

Fritz just works her mouth like she's dying for another gulp of her Dr Pepper, but is afraid to reach for it in front of Nell. Instead, she jumps to her feet and races into the attendance office to find a student worker who will walk my class schedule and bring down my assignments, every last one. As she moves through the hallway outside, I can hear her huffing and puffing, surely because she hasn't had this much exercise in centuries.

Nell rolls her eyes at me. "Incompetent cow," she mutters.

And in that moment, I begin to fall head over heels in love with Nell Zellers.

24

~

Schizophrenia is not a preventable disease.
It is a bullet traveling from an already fired gun.

We have to haul Nell's elliptical trainer through the back door in four different pieces, the damn thing's so heavy. But the trainer's not the only thing I get stuck lugging in. Nell brings her favorite saucepans and her framed Diego Rivera signed print and about nine tons of clothes. Sweaters, jackets, slacks galore. And heels—red, blue, tweed, patent, suede, toeless. I'm about to tease her—*Who do you think you are, Imelda Marcos?* But she seems so serious about needing it all, I just head back out to her

Toyota, wondering how so much crap could have fit into such a tiny little car.

Nell makes a special trip back to her house for her cockatiel and puts him right in the kitchen, where the sunlight is the warmest.

"There you go, Cockamamie," she says, smiling at her pet, which has a bright yellow head and an orange spot on his cheek like he's blushing. "Talk too much, and it's only three steps to the oven."

"I'll *roast* ya," Cockamamie whistles in a high-pitched slur. "*Roast* ya."

The whole scene makes me laugh. But while Nell's standing there, talking to the bird, I suddenly see them—all those broken pieces of fishing line, dangling from the ceiling, glistening like slender icicles in the sunlight. I think of the missing mermaids, still wrapped up in a blanket in the trunk of the Tempo. And Florida—I could practically pass out, the fumes from the memory of that vacation are so strong. There it is, the burn of salt water up my nose, and Mom saying, "We'll take them. *All* of them. We're just alike, me and Aura..."

What's wrong with me? How can I be standing here laughing like everything is hunky-dory, a-okay? How selfish can one jerk really be?

I have no idea what they're doing to her, my mother. I mean, Nell says she put Mom in a home—but like what? Like a nursing home, where old people are allowed to sit in their piss and shit and grow bedsores and beg for a sip of water? That kind of home?

I want to puke or scream or pass out or die. Instead, I excuse myself and head back toward my bedroom. I do, after all, have roughly forty-three million hours of homework to finish—and the entirety of *The Scarlet Letter* to read. Criminy.

My geometry book's spread open on my bed, and I'm giving the first problem what feels like the fiftieth try when I hear it—this rattle. It's unmistakable, you know? *Rattle-bang, clunkerty-clunk.* I raise my head to look out my window that is still engulfed by the same awful garden of crazy flowers that have swirled across my bedroom walls for years. Sure enough, on the street beyond the glass, there it is, a red p.o.s. with blue fenders.

Janny Jamison.

I try to turn back to my proof, reading and re-reading the lesson. (Jeez. Surely somebody's written a math book that can explain triangles in English. I mean, they're *triangles.* Why are they suddenly so difficult?) But, *rattle-bang, clunkerty-clunk,* the engine starts to grow louder, closer.

"Doesn't she have anything better to do?" I mumble as I crane my neck. While I'm staring out my window, she passes by again. But even as I ask it, I'm not annoyed. Seeing her circling through my neighborhood makes my heart overflow. When I touch the corner of my eye, my fingertip turns wet.

"Who the hell *is* that?" Nell asks, stomping into my room and pressing her face against my window. "You don't have a stalker, do you?"

"You never left," I blurt as Nell squints at the street.

"You could have left town when Mom moved out, gotten away from everything that hurt, but you didn't."

Nell gets this horrified look, like I've just accused her of trying to kill Mom with her bare hands. "Some things—some things you just always *are,*" she says quietly. "No matter how much time's passed. No matter how pissed you've been, how disappointed. I'll always be her mother."

I nod as the clunkerty-clunk comes back again, for the four millionth time.

The p.o.s. pauses, idling at the curb. But Janny—she's not just driving by for something to do. She's not driving to soothe her son. Janny's come because she doesn't know any of it—doesn't know about the red and blue swirling ambulance lights or that I talked to Fritz earlier that morning or that I practically gave myself a hernia hauling all my grandmother's shit into my house. Janny thinks that Mom is still here. Janny's come to help me.

"That's no stalker," I finally tell Nell, who's glaring through the window. "That's actually—" I almost choke on the words. "It's my best friend." I stand and hurry through my bedroom door. And Nell is curious, or still a little worried, maybe, so she follows at my heels. But she stays on the porch as I run across the front lawn.

"Janny," I call out, waving as the p.o.s. starts to take off again. "Janny!"

She slams the brakes, which are apparently wearing out, because the car skids into the middle of the road. She sticks her head out of the driver's side window as I step off the curb. Her motherly concern gets a watercolor smear of annoyance on it, and I figure that's because she's just remembered the last time we actually spoke.

I stop just short of her window, hide my hands as I cross my arms over my chest. Wish, for a minute, I could shove my whole stupid face down one of the pockets of the Nell-style slacks I'm still wearing.

"She's okay," I manage.

"Yeah, but for how long?" The way she screws her face up, you'd think her words tasted like a fistful of raw red onion.

"She's in a hospital, actually," I say. "Professional help galore. Are you?"

"Am I what?"

"Okay."

"I don't really know what you mean," Janny says, pushing some greasy, flyaway hairs from her eyes.

"You really did move out? From your parents' place?"

She hesitates, nods her head slowly. "We were at each other's throats so bad, I'm actually not sure if I stormed out or they kicked me out." She shrugs. "I've got an apartment behind the Kum & Go. It's not the Shangri-la, but it's all right."

"Is Ace helping at all? At least sending money, or something?"

She frowns. "What are you, retarded?"

"What about work?"

Janny rolls her eyes. "Who made you the chief of the baby police? I shampoo hair at Super Cuts, all right? Woman downstairs from me has a kid, too. We stagger our schedules so we can sit for each other."

I stare at her hands, already red and broken-out from washing hair all day long. Glance through the back window at the baby sleeping soundly.

"What happens when she moves, your neighbor? What happens when you *can't* juggle schedules?" I ask. "You need your diploma."

She snorts out a laugh. "I need a lot of things. To win the lottery, for starters."

"If I help you look after your kid—" I start, inching my toes closer to the car.

"Ethan," Janny corrects. "And I don't need a sitter, you know. I'm fine."

"No, that's not—If I help you study, would you get your GED?"

"Why?"

Because, I want to tell her, *the whole time we've been friends, I've always been the one who was drowning. The one asking you to keep my head above water. You were never afraid of the ocean.*

"I think maybe our friendship was a little one-sided," I say. "I think you were there for me for a long time, and when you needed somebody, I was AWOL."

Janny tilts her head; a ray of midmorning sun washes the shadows off her face. "What the hell, Ambrose?" she asks through that pit-bull expression of hers. "You come out to my car to write some schmaltzy-paltzy Hallmark card?"

I narrow my eyes at her. "Maybe I did, you dumb-ass," I say, which gets her to smile.

She puts her head down on the steering wheel and laughs. It's a good sound. Pretty—like piano music.

25

~

Postmortem brain tissue research is proving to be very important in the study of schizophrenia. And because the brain is removed from the back of the skull, there is no disfigurement—which, if you really dig open-casket funerals, is a great big (though highly morbid) bonus.

"I don't understand what the problem is," Nell's snapping at me as cars honk all around us. She's taking me to school, no more driving for me until I get my license, tsk-tsk.

"This is very simple," she insists, blaring her horn at an ancient station wagon. She leans out the window and screams, "The gas is on the *right*," at some poor gray-haired, white-knuckled driver.

Oh, yeah. And I'm the one who shouldn't be driving.

"I don't know—" I say, biting down on my thumbnail.

"What's there to know?" Nell shouts. "You like to draw. You're talented. Just like your mother." She must feel me cringe, because she says, "That's not a bad thing, Aura. You're talented like your mother. Wear it like a Girl Scout badge, all right?"

But I can't. She should understand. It's not like you can just turn a page and *poof!* A magical happy ending pops into view. You don't carry this all-encompassing dread around, you don't look at your mother absolutely convinced that *this is a mirror, this is who I'll be someday, nuts, nuts, nuts,* and then discard that thought in one afternoon. You can't, all right?

Correction: *I* can't.

"You let me sit in that damned meeting with that horrible *counselor* of yours, and you never once mentioned anything about the accelerated arts and letters program. You made me find out about it by listening to the old messages on your machine?"

"I don't—I just don't want—"

"Just because a couple of artists throughout history have had schizophrenia, that doesn't mean *you* will. That's ridiculous, Aura," she tells me. "I'm sure there were bankers and farmers who had schizophrenia, too. And lawyers and secretaries and manicurists..."

She is so pushy, I can seriously understand why she had so much trouble with my mother.

"...and trash collectors and doctors and zoo keepers," Nell goes on. "Does that mean you don't want to be any of those things when you grow up?"

When I grow up? Gag. I'd just as soon talk to Fritz.

"You try to stifle your creativity, all you're going to wind up doing is hating yourself. You'll wind up being boring," Nell insists, rolling her eyes. "For God's sake, whatever you do, just don't be boring."

"Let me out here," I snap.

"I'm taking you to the front door."

"Let me out here," I shout. Instantly, Nell veers to the curb. Horns blare and tires squeal on the pavement behind her.

"I'm not letting go of this," Nell shouts at me as I throw open the door of her Toyota. "It's too important. You're *taking* art."

I slam the door and rush off down the street. I know what I saw happen to Mom. And it got worse the more she painted. That *Bedroom in Arles* on her wall, it sucked her dry. It bled her, stole her health, like meth or booze. Nell doesn't know everything. If I do what she wants, I'll die. Can't she see that? I'll *die*. I've already got two generations before me afflicted by the same madness. And the thing they both had in common is that *they were both artists.* I can't help it. These thoughts are like a dirt path I've worn through the grass by taking the same shortcut every day. And once you've taken a shortcut, who can ever bear to go the long way around again?

As I near the Circle, I start to get a little queasy, because I figure word has traveled fast. I expect voices to trail off when I approach. Hands to cup mouths. Whispers to dance through the air like tiny butterflies with translucent wings.

Here she comes, they'll all say, *the one whose mom is wacko. The one whose mom even ran her father off. He couldn't take it anymore. Just look at her, how she walks, how she talks, how she fidgets. I'll bet the reason her father doesn't want her around is that he's afraid. Because, just watch, everyone will find out sooner or later, she's loony, too—or she will be, she—*

I straighten my back, the same way I figure Janny would if she knew she was gossip-fodder. *So they'll whisper when they see you, I* tell myself. *So what?* I decide to pretend that they're all whispering because I've just been through some miraculous thing—I've emerged as the lone survivor of the worst plane crash ever, or have rescued twelve dying kittens from a burning apartment building, or have found the cure for cancer living in an old wad of chewing gum on the bottom of my sneaker. I will pretend that they give me the big tennis-ball eyes because they're completely amazed.

Except they don't. Everybody's just talking amongst themselves, clustering and smoking, and nobody cares. My appearance doesn't exactly bring the goings-on of the Circle to a screeching halt. I don't even bring a momentary hiccup. Nobody even *looks* my way—well, one of them does.

Jeremy's got his hair pulled into a ponytail today, so it doesn't whip into his eyes. He stares at me like a boy watching a movie: *Wonder what will happen next.*

I want to say something to him. Jesus, just fucking *hello* or something. Maybe, *Am I some kind of asshole or what?* But I lose my guts, duck my chin into my chest, and sprint straight out of the Circle, toward Crestview's back entrance.

I have to pass the art room to get to my locker. I love the way the hallway smells just outside it—all pasty, dusty, and cool, like a fresh chunk of clay. I stand behind the door, peeking into the room.

The art teacher's got big wire glasses and an enormous white beard that makes an upside-down triangle down to the middle of his chest. The kids call him Grandpa Smurf. There's laughter when a pot collapses on the wheel in the back of the room.

I can hear feet behind me. The clopping of hard-soled shoes puts me in gear, because I figure it's a teacher—*Now, now, no loitering, you little gypsy. Off to class, or better yet, until the morning bell rings, why don't you head on to the library?* But just as I'm taking that first step, I see them. Blue cowboy boots with stars.

"Hey!" the Freak shouts.

"Hey, back," I mumble.

"Did you drop Bio or something?" She frowns. I notice she hasn't had a haircut in a while, and this morning, her daisy petal hair is standing out even more than usual.

"No," I shrug.

"What do you think, I'm gonna to carry you the rest of the semester?" she screeches.

I blink at her. "I hadn't thought—"

"I've done *all* the lab work since you've been gone. I'm *not* gonna to let you get credit for my work. Neither is Wickman. And I'm *not* gonna spend the rest of the semester tutorin' you to get you back on track. So don't even ask."

As she lays into me, I imagine that we're not in the

hallway at all, but an autopsy room. I'm stretched out on a carving table, a giant "Y" drawn on my naked chest where she's going to hack into me, head shaved in the back where she's going to pull out my brain. Angela's wearing her butcher's coat, all blood splattered. "I *knew* you'd never help me with this," she says, tugging on a pair of latex gloves. "Gonna make me do it all by myself."

"I'm so sorry," I say sarcastically. As I sit up, I purposefully knock Angela's tray of dissecting knives onto the floor. "I didn't mean to bother you with this. I won't trouble you anymore." I swing my legs and hop off the table.

"Where are you goin'?" she screeches. "I got dibs, remember?"

"The hell you do," I say. I throw my T-shirt on and stomp out of the autopsy room.

I'm laughing, thinking of it, and that just pisses the Freak off even more. But I have to admit, I never thought Frieson could look as beautiful as she does at this moment, frowning at me and shouting, "I mean, it Aura. You're *not* my responsibility." The way she's yelling at me for such trivial crap, it sort of makes me feel like life might actually, honest-to-God become normal.

26

~

When admitted, your schizo relative will be given a complete psychiatric and physical exam. Poked, prodded, sucked, interrogated, drained. And you wonder why they're not grateful to see you when you show up for your visit, a strained grin plastered across your cheeks like you're a yellow happy face?

Nell goes to visit Mom. She goes alone, on a Saturday, and comes back late in the afternoon. I'm at the kitchen table with Janny, who's filling out a bunch of enrollment papers for the GED program at the community college. All three of us—Janny, Ethan, and I—jump like cartoon cats when Nell comes tearing through, looking like she's been crying. She stomps down the hall slamming doors.

Janny shakes her head at me in such a sad way that I drop my head into my hands and wish I could melt, like a stick of butter. Melt in one of those *all the king's men just couldn't put her back together again* kind of ways.

By the time Nell drafts me as her sous-chef for our dinner spread, her face isn't so bright red and she seems to have calmed down. "You should go see her, Aura," she says. "She was asking about you."

I flinch, stop chopping up a stalk of celery for the soup. It's like Nell's ripped the knife out of my hand and stabbed me in the heart.

"You should go," Janny chimes in. She's still at the table, pouring over her scheduling worksheets. Ethan's asleep, his face pressed against her chest. "I'll go with you if you want. I wouldn't go in her room—I'd give you guys privacy—but I'll drive you there and wait in the lobby for you. Moral support and all."

God love her, it's as nice an offer as I'll ever get. But the whole idea of seeing Mom freaks me out worse than *not* seeing Mom had, the day she'd tried to water our no-longer-existent rose bushes. The same day I'd found Mom at the theater behind the art museum, watching an imaginary play.

What could she possibly have to say to me? *Me*—the one who got her locked away? What kind of hate will spill out of her mouth? Or maybe even worse—what if she doesn't talk to me at all? What if she's completely done with me?

I mean, a fight is one thing. And maybe, okay—so maybe, I think as I'm staring at Janny, a fight you can get over. But being put away because of your own kid? That's another matter entirely.

I let the whole thing drop.

Janny, on the other hand—

"I think you should go see her," she tells me the very next time she comes over. She's gotten a job answering phones at the administration office of the community college and is thinking about staying on once she passes the GED, studying something ultra-practical like dental tech. She's looking better, too—her hair is thickening up and her thighs are finally thinning down. And I love how great everything is going for her, but I swear, I could kick her out of my kitchen for being so good at giving me such grief.

"I'm going to go," I tell her. "She's my mother. I can't avoid her the rest of my life."

"*Exactly,*" she says. "What're you doing this afternoon?"

I drop back in my chair and let out this monster of a sigh. It's so loud, I wake Ethan. He starts getting all squirmy in his stroller. Janny instantly starts to rock it with her foot, still staring right at me. She raises an eyebrow.

"Shopping," I say, making the legs of my chair scream as they scrape across the linoleum.

"Shopping," Janny repeats, shaking her head as she watches me grab my jacket, like I've just told her my dream in life is to fly solo to the moon.

"I don't know about this," Janny says when we get back from Walmart. But I'm like a soldier, marching down the hall toward my room with all my purchases. I'm completely unstoppable.

"Seriously," Janny insists as I start spreading new drop cloths over my bed and my dresser. "This has been here forever," she goes on, touching an enormous lady bug that scurries up a polka-dotted daisy petal. "What's your mom going to think when she comes home?"

I pry open the lid of an eggshell-tinted flat paint and pull a roller out of a cellophane wrapper.

"Don't you think this is *sad*?" Janny asks.

No, I don't, I think. *You try living here ten minutes—then tell me you think painting over this loony-as-a-bedbug garden is sad.* I pour paint into a tray and wet the roller. It drips onto a drop cloth as I try to hand it to her.

"Please don't," she says, so I turn around and start slapping on the paint myself.

At first, it feels good. Not desperate, like I'd been when I'd painted over the mural in mom's bedroom. Just fresh, you know? Like taking a real bath after about three solid years of camping. But too soon, my arms ache. I've covered up about half of one wall when my eyes go all bleary.

"I don't want to see her," I admit. "I can't help it. I wish I did, but I just *don't.* I mean, the way Nell looks when she comes home from trying to visit her—I don't think she's exactly having an easy time with the whole making-up routine, so why should I?"

"Because you're her kid."

I snort. "So what?"

"So—you're strong, okay? I hope Ethan turns out to be half as strong as you."

"Cut the crap," I tell her. "This isn't the corny part in the story when Mariah Carey starts singing 'Hero' in the background. Mom has to think I'm so, so selfish—"

"No way," Janny interrupts. "You're *hers.* It's different, the way you feel for your own kid. It's cheesy, but it's true. You understand what it's like, you know, to try to take care of another human being. Grace has got to know how hard it was for you to reach out to Nell. I mean, if Ethan ever did something like that for me, I'd be *proud.*"

My eyes turn into rain-drenched windows. "That's a dirty trick," I whisper.

"Just get it over with already, Aura," Janny says. She puts Ethan on the floor and takes up another roller for herself. "I don't want to listen to you moan about it forever." She starts slapping paint on an opposite wall.

I re-wet my own roller. For a while the only sound in the room is the slimy slap of wet paint on my walls. "Saturday," I finally say.

From the corner of my eye, I see Janny's roller stop.

"Next Saturday," I say. "I'll go."

27

~

Consider having a friend who is less directly involved come with you to the nuthouse. Your buddy can help you remain calm if you find you are on the brink of a breakdown yourself.

Resolutions—what a nice name for a loony bin—is housed in a brick building that sits at the end of a wide circle drive and is enveloped by enormous oak trees. By now, those trees have all lost their leaves. Their naked limbs look like skinny arms that join together in a circle. It's as if the oaks are holding their own séance, attempting to pull every last patient inside Resolutions back into reality. Hope they're more successful than I was.

Janny yanks the parking brake. She's singing under her breath like all is roses. I could smack her for it, actually.

I have on this fuzzy red sweater Mom always liked me in, but since it's wool, it feels like I'm drenched in the itching powder that WWII prisoners got tortured with. I've even put on some lipstick and perfume, but it's just so unlike me, it makes me feel a little like a mannequin.

While Janny pulls Ethan from his car seat, I twist myself out of her p.o.s. The air feels like breath from a just-opened freezer. I instantly hate everything about this place.

I grab my sloppy canvas bag from the backseat. It's lumpy from the trinket that I guess I've brought to bribe Mom. It seemed like a good idea yesterday. Now, I think maybe I ought to leave it out here.

But I don't.

Janny's pushing me forward, *come on, come on,* probably afraid I'll lose my guts. It's icy cold, but I'm sweating so much all the powder's melted off my face. I start to wish that I could be a puddle instead of a girl.

"She'll hate me," I tell Janny. "She's got to hate me."

"Shut up," Janny says. We're suddenly in the lobby and she's sitting in some awful plastic chair the color of rotten Brussels sprouts, jiggling Ethan on her knee. "We'll wait here. Go on."

My feet are moving, I'm walking toward Mom's room, but I think, *God, if you exist and you like me the teensiest little bit, you'll let me pass out so I won't have to endure this, her anger, her hate.*

I'm halfway down the hall when it occurs to me that Janny probably can't see me anymore from her chair in the lobby. I consider making a run for it. I start to think,

What if I just bolt and am never heard from again? Why can't that be a happy ending? Why can't it? But instead of sprinting, I'm looking inside her room, and there she is. Grace Ambrose.

And she is very much alive.

She's inside her room, painting. Not furiously, not like some crazed maniac. More like she used to, at the easel in front of her classroom. I just stand there watching, nerves prickling all over my skin.

"Hey," Mom says when she looks up. She rushes to me and gives me this hug—it's like she's juiced me or something, because tears instantly spring to my eyes. She's put some weight on, and she smells clean and young—God, she smells like the sun, you know? Like summer, even though Thanksgiving's already come and gone.

"Come here," she says. "I want to show you what I've been working on."

She drags me across the room. The familiar face that stares back at me from the canvas has Mom's long black hair. But it isn't Mom, not quite.

"It's me," I say. I chuckle. "It's me."

"I missed you," Mom says, wrapping her arms around my neck and kissing the back of my head. "If I can't have you in the flesh every day, I can at least have the next best thing."

It blows my mind—*missed me? She's not pissed? How can this be?*

"I missed your birthday, didn't I?" Mom says apologetically, her eyes glistening. And I can't believe it; I'm struck dumb, because she's acting like we're old friends. Some ties truly are like steel.

But I don't want her to be sad, so I'm opening my canvas bag and reaching inside. And I pull out one of our mermaids that I've rescued from the trunk of the Tempo. Clean and dust-free, with a fresh coat of glitter on the tail.

Mom attempts a smile, but it breaks. "You fixed it," she says, as she fights her tears.

"A little slice of home." I shrug. "Just until you get back. But we have to hang it properly."

"Of course," she says, playing along.

We climb onto her bed to hang the mermaid from the ceiling. As we bring our arms down, we stand staring at each other eye to eye.

"Thanks, Aura," she says.

For the first time in what seems like eons, my body doesn't feel so clenched, so hot. And suddenly, I realize that the dot out there on my horizon line—the same dot everything in my world points to, like in the one-point perspective sketches Mom taught me how to draw—it's not any old spot, you know. It's not some charcoal smudge. It's peace.

28

~

Schizophrenia is a disease that is greatly feared and not well understood. Most of what people think they know about schizophrenia is wrong.

We're in family therapy, which means we're preparing for Mom to come home. It also means that our family is a single living organism. It means the "patient" isn't my mom, but the entire brood. It means we are regularly visiting a shrink who refuses to take sides, even though Mom wants him to. It means we invite my dad to join us, and he refuses—big surprise. And, it means we are all learning to communicate, which seems pretty ridiculous to me.

We're also drawing a genogram. It's a fancy word for

a family tree. Actually, it's a family tree that doesn't just include birth and death dates, but all the horrible, embarrassing crap that you'd rather not ever write down at all—illnesses and divorces and resentments and breakups.

Yeah, family tree—*family* in this case meaning me, Mom, and Nell, though Mom's still not jazzed about the Nell part. Whenever the subject of her dad comes up, Mom practically goes into hysterics.

"You don't get to make up for what happened to him. You can't make up for that by being nice to me now," Mom screams.

"I don't want to," Nell tries to tell her. But Mom is so furious, I don't know why her rage hasn't swallowed her whole.

Family tree—when our therapist asks for the name of *my* father, I say, "There isn't one. Hasn't that gotten through to you by now?" But he makes me write it down anyway, which shows me how little the guy really understands.

After a particularly brutal session, our therapist (who smells like a weird combination of licorice and chicken lo mein, go figure) pulls me aside and says, "Your grandmother tells me you're hesitant to sign up for art class."

I already feel like a nail that's been hammered at from all sides. And I'm thinking, *Now? You want me to talk about this now?* So I get kind of snotty and I say, "You want me to put that on our genogram, too?"

He sighs and looks at me like I'm some mean-ass personal trainer that's wearing him out with wind sprints. "Look," he says. "You're a smart girl. I'm not going to patronize you. It's true—there are some ongoing studies that are examining the link between creativity and schizophrenia. But creativity in itself is not a *cause* of schizophrenia. A by-product, maybe—a positive side effect, perhaps, but you show no signs... Art class won't hurt you, Aura. I promise."

"Great. Got it," I say, but he grabs my arm.

"You don't seem convinced," he says, raising an eyebrow.

I just stare back. "Have you even looked at our genogram?" I ask him. "An artist and a writer, okay? Two stupid branches right above me. What am I *supposed* to think?" I turn away so that he can't see the tears that are coming, like two shiny babies insisting on being born.

He cocks his head. "Renoir, Annie Leibovitz, Raphael, Isadora Duncan, Steinbeck, Paul Newman, John Lennon, Toni Morrison—"

"What is this?" I interrupt.

"Artists, every single one. A bit rebellious and wild, some of them, but none with any kind of mental illness that I'm aware of. Shall I go on? Let's see," he says, rolling his eyes toward his widow's peak. "Clint Eastwood, Tony Bennett, Les Paul, Pearl Buck—"

"Are you making fun of me?" I snap.

"No," he shrugs. "The point is, Aura, the list of sane artists far outnumbers the list of unstable ones. I can tell you in all honesty there is no link between mental illness and the actual process of creating. Okay? None. I realize you have some concerns—rightly so—based on your family history. But art class *will not* hurt you, Aura."

I really don't know what to do—I guess I'm a little like a bird who's railed against her cage her whole life, only to cock her head to the side in confusion when somebody finally opens the door.

I hurry to catch up with Nell, who's always so emotional after our sessions, I figure she'd probably drive off without me.

At home, Nell's shining everything up—dusting and scrubbing and rearranging. She hangs some of Mom's finished paintings. She vacuums, she spit polishes. She buys new mirrors for the front hall and the bathroom.

She goes everywhere but Mom's room.

It looks exactly like it did the night the paramedics came, door closed so neither one of us has to address it.

Sometimes, though, avoiding something becomes more work than actually looking at it. So I finally turn the knob and step inside. I pick up all her scattered brushes, take down the paint-spattered curtains. Tear off her pillowcases, tuck the corners of fresh sheets beneath the mattress, and pull her covers up all tight and neat. Dust and vacuum; pick up all the crystals I'd used during my séance.

When I'm done, there's still the problem of Mom's mural. It continues to glow through the single coat of white paint I'd slopped up there in my lame attempt to just make it all go away. Mom had used so many of van Gogh's yellows that her wall now looks like a lamp with a filmy scarf thrown over it. I sigh, staring at it until my eyes start to feel foreign and sticky in my own head.

Art won't hurt you. Our therapist's words echo, like a voice in a shower stall. I mean, even the crappiest voice sounds good in a shower, you know? And right then, those words actually start to resonate in a melodic way. *Art won't hurt you.* I like the way that sounds.

Nell shows her work at December's First Friday Art Walk. I show up, too, wearing another Nell ensemble—the woman likes to shop for me, and who am I to discourage that? Tonight, it's an A-line dress, a funky orange number, which is retro enough to actually fit in with the self-portraits Nell took of herself back (as one might say) in the day. She's even loaned me a few of the political buttons that had filtered down to the bottom of her jewelry box, the way raisins work their way down toward the bottom of the cereal box as it's being shipped from the warehouse to the grocery store.

It's a pretty stuffy affair, frankly, with a bunch of snoots (mostly from the university) toting wine glasses around and staring at Nell's life like it's just an object. Just some two-dimensional images. I feel like twisting my hair into a bun, sauntering up to them, and telling them to get their pseudo-intellectual asses out of my grandmother's studio. Take their judgmental attitudes somewhere else, because this is my life, too, that they're looking at, not just Nell's, because we're all so tangled, the three of us. Me and Nell and Mom.

And suddenly, I know exactly what to do with Mom's bedroom wall.

When Nell and I finally get back to the house, I crack open a small can of green—can't rely on little tubes of acrylic and oil, because what I want to do is far too big. My arms feel wobbly as I dip a brush inside the can, and my heart beats so hard, it hurts. I press the brush against the wall. *Am I really going to do this?*

"Art won't hurt you," I tell myself.

I lick my dry lips and put a shaky hand against the wall, make a long sweeping horizontal line. It looks so pitiful up there, but I hear Mom's voice: *Don't get frustrated at your first line on the page—of course that first line doesn't look like anything. It won't until you shade it in and get the shadows right.*

I open a can of blue, dip my brush, mix, stroke. My hand starts to even out, like I've been miraculously cured of Parkinson's. My strokes grow quicker, more sure. I mix, I blob, I use my fingertips when the brush just isn't doing what I want it to.

I grab one of Mom's charcoals to help me sketch the faces. I've got some of Nell's photographs to help me with this part. As I draw, I keep my eye on the self-portraits Nell snapped three decades ago, and the images she captured of my mother when Mom was about my age.

I draw their young faces, and mine, too, using a mirror, remembering other lessons Mom taught me, about how far apart the eyes are, and how to put shadows around noses, and then I'm painting again, long hair, arms, three chests, but one tail—one long shimmering green mermaid tail. Because we are all three different, but so much the same. We all come from the same skin, the same history.

It's been so long—a whole century, it feels like—since I've lost myself in a painting. A real painting and not some sketch thrown down in a journal, only to be tossed under my bed in embarrassment. I mean, all I've done is pick up a paintbrush, but what I *feel* is that I've been away so long, a weary traveler, stranger in a strange land, and here I am, I've just pulled my car into the drive, and I'm running up the front walk, and I can barely even calm down enough to get my key in the front door, because I've made it.

I'm home.

29

~

Having a support system is essential for the survival of a fruitloop.

The thing about elliptical trainers and birds and shoes and big red jasper necklaces is that they go out as easily as they come in. We pack up all Nell's stuff the day before we're supposed to go pick Mom up from Resolutions. Seems stupid now to have brought so much for what feels like such a short stay. I figure she's the kind of woman who packs fourteen trunks of junk just to go out of town for the weekend. We cart it all back to Nell's house—everything but the trainer and Cockamamie, who Nell stares at sadly that last night as she drinks a rather large vodka tonic.

I think I could maybe make some crack about not wanting to have to start taking care of her, too, or about how I sure hope she didn't catch alcoholism from staying next door to the Pilkingtons. But Nell doesn't look like she'd find much humor in anything tonight—and besides, that's really not so funny, anyway.

I ought to join her at the table, but I wind up lingering in the doorway, fidgeting like some cafeteria nerd who can't get up enough guts to ask a table of kids if it's okay to sit down.

"Her meds are working," I blubber. "There's no reason for her to be at Resolutions anymore."

Nell nods and runs her fingers through her stark white hair. She looks really old, like she's suddenly feeling as though her life is an anchor.

"Did you sign up for that art class yet?" Nell asks.

I shrug.

Nell ages another forty years in that moment. She sighs over her ice cubes as she slurps down the rest of her drink.

When we finally do pick Mom up, she lets Nell carry her suitcase. I carry the mermaid, the fishing line hanger twisted around my index finger. We put it all in the trunk of Nell's Toyota and pile in like we're getting on a bus. Like we've never seen each other before; we're all a bunch of kids headed out to our very first summer camp and we're terrified and want to seem tough but also don't want to accidentally bump anyone, because we just might get killed.

We don't say anything on the drive home. I stare at the dead brown grass along the edge of the street.

Mom wants to unpack on her own, so I help Nell with her crazy elliptical trainer. I buckle Cockamamie's cage into the passenger's seat of the Toyota, and turn to find Nell giving me this funny stare. "You want me to come with you?" I ask. "Help you unload it at your house?"

She shakes her head. "Call me tomorrow and let me know how everything's going," she says. But it sounds funny. Desperate, you know? Like a tiny voice in a well begging for help.

"Okay," I say.

"No—not just okay. This isn't over for me. I'm not going anywhere. I'm not going to turn my back on you and Grace, all right?"

"Okay," I say again, but my voice is huskier because I mean it, this time. "Really, though—that nurse you paid for's coming over to check on us every day, and I'll see you at the studio on Saturday, so—"

"*No,*" Nell says, shaking her white hair forcefully. "You call me tomorrow. And every day after that. And if you don't, I'm going to be the one calling *you.* I'm not going anywhere. And don't you ever be afraid to tell me anything, you hear?"

I have to stifle a laugh, because my mind turns into an old clip of the Jackson 5, little Michael belting out, "I'll Be There."

"Deal," I say, and watch Nell pull away.

I'm still standing in the driveway when Mom comes bursting out of the house and grabs me around my neck, hugging me so hard she practically lifts me right off the ground.

"I saw the mural," she says. "It's really beautiful."

But my heart's still limping away inside me, because I already know what's coming next.

"You didn't *have* to put Nell in it," she says, looking at me sideways, kind of all-knowing, like a mother in an old-fashioned sitcom who's getting after her daughter for sneaking out the night before to go to the sock hop with the coolest cat on campus.

"I kinda did, though," I tell her.

"So I guess you're going to tell me you like her."

"She's not half bad."

Mom snorts and shakes her head.

"She is trying, you know," I say. "You could try, too."

"Yuck," Mom says. We stand there a minute before she says, "Quit looking at me like that. It's not like it's going to happen in the next ten minutes, all right?" But the way she wraps her arm around my shoulders as she leads me into the house makes me feel like it actually will.

30

~

If a set of genes really does exist to predispose a person to becoming a schizo, it is possible that those same genes also rev a person's creativity, actually helping them to survive in the long run.

The next day, I fill out a request for a change of schedule. I slip it into Fritz's box in the faculty office. Next semester, I will not be taking Keyboarding like I said I would last spring. God, *Keyboarding,* the world's biggest snoozer of a class, with the world's most ancient teacher, Mr. Brown, who is so old, I swear he doesn't breathe out air, but dust.

I am taking Art I. Goodbye, Mr. Brown, Dust Breath. Accelerated arts and letters program, here I come.

Part of me wants to skip all the way to the stairs.

Another part wants to drag my feet. I don't know that this dread will ever completely heal.

I pause outside the art room and peek in. Today, it smells like a cave—like shelter, protection. Grandpa Smurf has taped a sign to his door: *One Week Till All School Exhibition At Art Museum!* In the back of the room, a girl with a mop of green curls and a boy with no hair at all are acting like some giggly two-headed creature, tangling their fingers in a bowl of papier-mâché paste—criminy, it's almost like some old scene from *Ghost* or something.

But I just keep staring at them.

I remember the skateboard I'd propped in my closet before Nell, in her cleaning frenzy, could shrug and toss it out. My fingers start to itch.

31

~

A maintenance dosage is the lowest dosage at which the schizo is stable and can actually almost pass for a sane person.

Mom's sweating when we roll to a stop outside of the art museum. But not in a sick way, not this time. She takes a deep breath and shakes her hands like she's trying to flick water off of them. "How bad was it?" she asks, her voice quivering a little with nerves.

I shrug. "It wasn't *that*—"

"Oh, no," Mom groans, putting her head in her hands. Because she's back to being able to read me. I can't lie to her. She knows just by looking at me how horribly she acted at the art museum the day she swore her student's drawing was actually on fire. And even though I feel rotten about not being able to conceal this, I love the fact that she's back. Love it so much, I grab her hand and squeeze.

"Just tell the curator about the meds," I say. "And therapy, and the genogram—"

"Sure. And simple as that," she says, snapping her fingers, "I've got my job back." She climbs out, and so do I, pulling a painted skateboard out with me. I'm glad she's too nervous about the interview to ask what I'm doing with it.

"Good luck," I tell her.

"Luck. Hah," she says, shaking her head.

Mom disappears inside the museum, and I sit beneath the maple closest to the sidewalk. The longer I wait, the more my heart starts feeling like it's been saturated with liquid tenderizer. I don't even know if he'll come today.

But he does. He flies down the sidewalk on another board, followed by his friend with the toucan nose. And when Jeremy sees me, he sends the friend away. Says something all ultra-cool, *Catch up with you later,* like it's no big deal.

And maybe, I catch myself thinking, it's not. Maybe Jeremy's already broken up his Aura collection, all those tidbits he told me he'd saved when we were in Mom's drawing class together. Maybe he's trashed it, because come on, in a way, rose petals pressed between the pages of a book are romantic, but then again, it's just pieces of a dead plant, right? Isn't that what being sentimental boils down to? Hanging onto worthless crap?

Just like on the day he'd given me the board in the first place, I feel as sturdy as a tower made of ice cream scoops. I'm melting, going clammy in my sneakers and under my arms. My palms are as sticky as Post-its.

But I knew this would probably happen. So I pull my butterfly from the pocket of my coat. Okay, not a real butterfly, but a piece of orange construction paper folded into one—an origami copy. *Open me* is scrawled down the butterfly's body in thick block letters (à la *Alice in Wonderland*), not that Jeremy really needs the instruction, because my handwriting spills back and forth across the wings. Just looking at the butterfly, it's obvious that I'd written Jeremy a note before folding it. God, just like some awful girly-girl who spends every single one of her class periods writing messages to slip in her BFF's locker.

I've poured everything out in this note—about Mom becoming the shell of herself, and that fire at the museum and why I shouted those awful things at him, and even, oh, God, Nell and my dad and Brandi and Carolyn and even—*Jeez, is this too much?*—how Jeremy's kiss had made me feel so free in the midst of a life that was starting to shred to pieces. And maybe, I've written, if he still wants to, if I am not the biggest jerk on the planet, just a minor one, then maybe we could be like those geezers who find their high school crushes on the Internet after being apart for the better part of a century. Only we wouldn't have to wait years—we'd be lucky that way.

Maybe, I've written, *we could really be beautiful.*

I put the butterfly-shaped note, which has one of my

deepest wishes tattooed across its wings, onto his skateboard. I've painted the board all funky and modern. Instead of a scene, though, I've created wild shapes and splashes of black and orange—the up-close pattern of a monarch wing—hoping that he won't hate it, spray paint over it the instant he takes it home. I pull out a dispenser of Scotch tape from my coat pocket and stick the butterfly down, so it won't go flying off. Before I can chicken out, I give the skateboard a gentle push.

When Jeremy bends to pick up the butterfly, I disappear into the museum. I can't stand to be around when he reads it.

32

~

Recovery from schizophrenia is an oxymoron. You don't get over being schizo like you get over a cold. There's no cough syrup or topical cream or even a pill that can eliminate the schizo from your brain. But you and your caregivers can work together to monitor your condition and even come up with a plan of action should your symptoms come roaring back, exploding in your family members' faces like pipe bombs. Blam!

Saturday, and for the first time since that day at the art museum when Mom scrawled those oddball words on her blackboard *(PEPPER, PET)*, it really does feel like a weekend. A real, live, breathing *weekend*, with pancakes for breakfast. And two midmorning classes at the art museum, because the curator has a definite sympathy bone for what she calls Mom's "artistic temperament." But to be safe, just two classes on Saturday. For now.

I'm standing on a ladder, making cloud bursts with every breath as I try to untangle the white twinkle lights. I might not have any homework left to do, but these stupid lights pose a tougher problem than any geometry book could cook up. *What sadistic s.o.b. thought these things up anyway,* I wonder as I loosen a knot in the wire, but I'm really not annoyed at all.

Actually, I'm cutting it pretty close, with Christmas looming like a giant wad of mistletoe just an inch above my head. Local news has been broadcasting from the mall for the past three days. From the looks of it, the line to see Santa stretches from Sears past the food court.

I hope we get a tree, too—not a dead one, chainsawed for a week's worth of good times. But one of those small table-sized jobs, the kind in a pot, that you plant in the backyard after the holidays. Yeah, a small one would be nice—a few ribbons, some miniature glass snowflakes.

Maybe Nell could even come over. Not for the whole day, but for a while.

Next door, Scooter starts barking—that happy yip of a young dog wanting to play.

"*Hush,*" Mrs. Pilkington scolds as she makes a beeline for the shed out by the back fence. She pops the lid off the metal trash can and makes this guttural groan, like she's suddenly in intense pain, like someone's punched her in the gut.

Her back door flaps open, and Joey emerges just in time to see his mom attack the trash can. But the can doesn't clang as glass bottles rattle around inside. When Mrs. Pilkington kicks the can across the yard, it's obviously empty. Hollow. No whiskey.

"Come on, Mom," Joey says quietly. "I know how hard it is."

Even though I expect her to, Mrs. Pilkington doesn't shake her head and say something parental, like *Who do you think you are? I used to change your diapers. You don't tell me what to do. I'm your mother.* She just lets Joey put his arm around her and lead her inside.

As the trash can rolls to a stop, I turn my eye toward the burn pile in the center of my own backyard. An enormous sigh escapes my chest, like I'm some cloud-sized helium balloon that's just popped. Because even though Mrs. Pilkington really does have to get rid of the thing that she loves, the thing that she believes makes her function, *I* don't. Because Mom and I have replaced the canvases I torched. Because we bought all the sketchbooks and the charcoals and the watercolor paper I'll need next semester in Art I. And because I'm writing new poems, putting them together into a kind of mini chapbook, in a deal I've made with Kolaite for extra credit. (God knows, after all my class cutting, my grades need all the help they can get.)

I don't have to give it up, any of it. Not the writing. Not the drawing. And neither does Mom. And that makes me feel like we've both been given some sort of second chance, you know? Some sort of *begin again.*

I hear the muffled sound of our phone ringing from inside the house.

"Aura!" Mom shouts, throwing open the back door. "It's for you."

I climb down from the ladder, hope like a blowtorch in my gut.

"It's Jeremy," she says, then tosses me that sideways sitcom-mom look. "Is this Jeremy-from-drawing-class Jeremy?"

"You remember," I say.

"Why would I forget?"

I push past her and pick up the phone, trying desperately to play it cool, even though I really want to squeal like some awful girly-girl.

"Hey, Jeremy," I say.

"Yeah, listen, so about this autobiography you gave me the other day..." As Jeremy's voice tingles inside my ear, I wander over to the kitchen table. I sit in the same chair Mom used to flop into while I fixed her lunch, looking like an empty jean jacket.

Above, the mermaids closest to the sliding glass door sway a little as Mom slams the door shut. But they are no longer cracked or dusty or lifeless. They all have fresh coats of paint. Broken fins have been repaired. New glitter twinkles across their scales like untouched snow. Because Mom and I are fixing the mermaids as we hang them back up, giving them all back their magical sparkle, one by one.

epilogue

~

Mom insists we take Janny and Ethan on our summer vacation—"To take the sting off Nell being there," she says, rolling her eyes at me. Sometimes the way she keeps resisting Nell gets a little tiresome—almost like she's doing it just to prove her point. But Nell refuses to get discouraged. The two of them are a little like bulldogs, each of them planting their feet and refusing to budge their strong, meaty bodies. At least they're not growling and baring their teeth.

It's a strange brood to have on a road trip, you know.

We have to stop at the A&P for diapers for Ethan and Aspercreme for Nell. And we all pester Mom about her meds in that way families can pinch each other without anybody really getting all that pissed off.

As the Tempo swirls down gray ribbons of highway, closer and closer to the Florida state line, I start to wonder about the guy who carved all our mermaids. I wonder if he still has that souvenir shop, and is still, every single day, digging the same face out of driftwood, dropping every finished piece into the same galvanized tub, *Mermaids $2.* And I wonder if he ever got it right, the shine on those carvings. Wonder if he ever saw her again, his ocean mermaid, or if she disappeared for good.

But we're not going back to his piece of Florida. We've moved on. So I guess I'll never really know about what became of him or his tiny little sculptures.

When we cross the bridge at Jewfish Creek and finally arrive in Key Largo, the surroundings completely blow my mind. The breeze here sounds tinny, twangy, like calypso music. And it smells like a piña colada.

"Go straight to the beach, Nell," I say.

"No way," Janny argues, because, with all his squirming and diaper changes, Ethan's worn her as flat as a pencil that's just drafted an entire novel. "Let's go to the hotel. *Please.*"

"A hotel? When there's *this*?" I ask, pointing out the window. Palm leaves wave hello. Coconuts tumble. "It *exists.* White sands, blue water. Look, Janny. A *real* tropical paradise. We didn't get to see this when we were kids. And you want to go to some crummy hotel?"

Janny sighs. "Fine," she mumbles, even though I can tell, from the way her eyes light up, that she's excited to be here, too. We've arrived in another world. The kind of place that proves fairy tale lands really do exist, after all.

"Aura!" Nell shouts, because as soon as we hit the shoreline, I throw the passenger's side door open. "Wait till I stop the damn car."

"What's wrong with you?" Janny snaps, and Mom starts getting after me, too—I've got three mothers shouting out a chorus of *you'll get hurt*, but I don't care. I'm out of the car and I'm running right up to the white frothy fringes.

Only I don't stop there. I just keep going, ankle deep, knees soaked, my laughter pouring out and my arms flapping oddly, like I'm a seagull and this is where I was always meant to be.

I immerse myself, open my eyes beneath the surface. The water's so clear, it really could be someone's swimming pool. A big, blue swimming pool full of tiger-striped fish. And the salt water in my eyes doesn't even sting, like I expected it to.

On this vacation, I can't get enough of the water. I buy snorkeling gear and flippers, which I figure make me look a little ridiculous. But I can't help it—I just want to go deeper beneath the surface, farther, touching the sea plants and rocks, exploring. I want to time-freeze everything I see, like my eyes are the shutters of one of Nell's cameras. There's poetry down here. And about a hundred different watercolors waiting to be painted.

When I finally do come up for air, my fingers aren't just pruned, but white and bloated on the tips—like every single one of them is covered in blisters. I pull my goggles off, laughing as I watch Janny in her floppy, to-the-knees white T-shirt cover-up, racing down the shore, screaming, "Ethan! Come back here!" But he just squeals that high-pitched little boy giggle, because he's got Janny's fearlessness.

Nell trails along behind them, snapping away with her camera. It's too bad she's using the old-fashioned Nikon—not a digital, but a camera with actual film—because I'd love to see what these pictures look like right this instant. They'll be amazing; I know they will. Nell's got such a knack for capturing people as they really are that I figure every time I see one of these photos, I'll be able to hear Ethan's high-pitched laughter all over again... even if, by that point, Ethan's old enough to have a goatee.

Nell lowers her camera and nods at a cluster of shirtless surfers. I glance at them, shrug a *so what?* But Nell winks and says, "Way out, kid." When I turn back, I realize, with shock waves traveling down my body like a hundred Slinkys racing down a flight of stairs, that the surfers are oogling me.

I touch the necklace at the base of my throat—two entwined wooden circles on a steel cord that I've been wearing for months, refusing to take it off to sleep or shower. I've actually got a tan line around it—the retired skateboard cut by Jeremy's hands—on the skin just beneath my clavicle. As I run my fingers over the circles, tracing their outline, I don't care enough about the surfers' attention to really even be flattered. I just chastise myself for trying to shove my torpedo boobs into some too-small-for-me black bikini.

Late in the afternoon, when the sun's reds begin to charge across the water, Mom and I grab our sketchbooks and beach chairs, carry them so far out, the ocean's all the way past our ankles. Mom's wearing her own soggy bikini—a kind of retro-looking number—her black ponytail blowing across her face. God, she looks so young—*Grace Ambrose, born April 3, 1970. And has there* ever *been anyone quite so alive?*

"Challenge," Mom tells me as she flips open her sketchbook, like she does every day at this time, when the light is perfect, the two of us battling for the best drawing. Just as I pick up one of my new pencils—a sapphire blue—I hear a snap behind my shoulder, and when I turn, I realize Nell's taken our picture. Before Mom can wave her off, Nell sticks her tongue out at her. Which actually makes Mom laugh—a little.

"And I'm off to happy hour," Nell announces triumphantly. She hurries up the coast in her fitted capris, toward the hotel lounge, like she's forty years younger than she really is. Age hasn't touched either of them, Nell or Mom.

The thing is—and Mom would never even consider the possibility of this being true—but really, she and Nell butt heads because they're so much alike. Everything from the shape of their angular faces all the way down to their eyes—not the color of them, but the way they work. The way those eyes *see*. And that's helping me to take a lot of the lingering fear factor out of blank canvases. *Nell's an artist, too.*

I mean, life's not flawless. It's not like I'm Goldilocks settling into the perfect setting, saying, *This is just right.* But as I'm sitting next to my mom, our hands poised on the pages in nearly identical angles, I have to say, *This feels so good*... I fill my lungs with sweet air as I try to decide what I'm going to sketch—one of the palms, leaves like a funky layered hairdo? The sailboat creeping dangerously close to a horizon line that looks like the edge of the entire world?

I stare down at my feet, at the skin that's a shade lighter because it's underneath the blue tint of the water. I wiggle my toes, disturbing the sand. For a moment the water clouds, reminding me of my first visit to Florida.

"You're not drawing," Mom says, singsong. "If you don't get started soon, I'll win."

I sigh, collapsing into the back of my beach chair. "There's just so much more, you know? Underneath the surface. When we came—the first time? I thought I'd see all the way to the bottom of the ocean. Sunken pirate ships and all."

By this point, Mom's pencil has stopped moving. "Why didn't you?"

I snort a laugh, thinking she's trying to be a smart-ass.

But she's looking at me like she wouldn't know sarcasm if it stung her like a jellyfish. She's being utterly serious.

"You don't *see* the ocean floor, Mom," I tell her. "It's not a fish bowl, all right? It's the ocean."

A crooked grin starts to tap dance into the side of her cheek. "Close your eyes."

"I'm not some little girl, Mom—" I start to protest.

"Let me tell you something, Aura," she says, in that same tone she uses in the front of her classroom. "There's another side to art, okay? The magical side. Sure, you have to start with something solid, copying images that already exist, that stand right in front of you. But the best artists? They draw not from the world, but from their imaginations. *That's* how you see the ocean floor, Aura. You dream it. You create it. You draw it."

I tense up a little, try to shrug her away.

"What have you drawn from your imagination since you painted that three-headed mermaid on my wall?" she asks with a raise of her eyebrow. "Hmm? Nothing, that's what."

"I had assignments, Mom—"

"Can it. Don't blame it on some art teacher. 'You had assignments.' You passed Art I with flying colors, drawing bowls of fruit and little wooden dolls." She sticks a finger in her mouth, like she's gagging herself. "You and I both know you could have been more creative. Come on," Mom insists. "Close your eyes."

My eye travels back up the shore, in the direction my

grandmother just disappeared. *Nell's an artist, too,* I remind myself. *Creative doesn't have to mean crazy. Right?*

I do what Mom suggests—as my eyelashes knit, the late afternoon sun gives the backs of my eyelids a red glow.

"Flick your tail," Mom says.

"My *tail*?" I moan, my eyes popping back open again. "What am I, eight?"

"Shut up," Mom says, leaning over the arm of her beach chair to cup my eyes with her palm. "Your tail," she repeats. "That beautiful mermaid tail you painted on my bedroom wall. Flick your tail and dive in—not into the waters of the Florida Keys, but inside *you.*"

"This is stupid," I mumble, but Mom's suggestion has made my mind explode. I swear, I can *feel* the cool water against my shoulders as I plunge in. Bubbles dance up my arms.

"Keep going," Mom whispers. "Speed up—faster than a shark. Deeper and deeper into your own creativity, your mind, your art."

I flick my imaginary tail again and fly through the waters, taking in the surroundings entirely through my skin, since my eyes are still closed. Deeper and deeper, just like Mom said. I brush past a tangle of seaweed. Schools of fish tickle my skin and scales as I speed past. The farther I swim into my imagination, the farther I get from any lingering fear. A squeal builds low in my belly, because I'm free.

My fingertips strike something mossy, ancient.

"You're there, aren't you?" Mom asks. "The ocean floor?"

I let out a murmur, because I'm not done yet. I don't have to stop here—and I burrow deeper still, squirm under the ocean floor, to a world never before explored. My own world.

"Go ahead, Aura," Mom whispers. "Draw what you see."

I open my eyes.

About the Author

Holly Schindler dove headfirst into her writing pursuits after obtaining an MA in English from Missouri (*Ma-zur-AH*) State University. Teaching private piano and guitar lessons to pay the bills quickly made her realize she wanted to write for the teens who filled her home with music. Having penned a pile of drafts that literally stretches to the ceiling, she is ecstatic to be releasing her first novel with Flux. She is a member of SCBWI, lives with a ridiculously spoiled Pekingese, and is firmly convinced that Springfield-Style Cashew Chicken is the ultimate writing fuel.

Interview with Holly Schindler

By Allie Costa

~

Ubiquitous blogger Little Willow (aka Allie Costa) put fingers to keys for a cyberspace chat with author Holly Schindler.

ALLIE COSTA: A Blue So Dark *studies the life of a girl who, as she turns from fifteen to sixteen, watches her once lively mother lose her grasp on reality as she is overwhelmed by schizophrenia. What prompted you to write about schizophrenia? How much research did you do into the condition before or while writing the book?*

HOLLY SCHINDLER: I've also always been interested in what *makes* a person creative. Why one person can write an entire volume of poetry while another just stares at the blue lines on a blank piece of notebook paper, unable to come up with a single rhyme. My interest in creativity really exploded in grad school... I taught a few courses while working on my master's, and I was amazed by the way some of my students could go on for half a class period about the meaning in a poem I'd bring in for discussion, while others would *just* read the literal surface-meaning, not probing any deeper, not really making any connections or seeing metaphors. But why *is* that? Why *do* some people look at everything literally, while others constantly see something more?

A Blue So Dark isn't autobiographical in that I didn't grow up with a mentally ill mother. But while I don't have any personal experience with schizophrenia, I didn't have to probe very deep into the subject of creativity to find out that many of our "great" artists (playwrights, poets, novelists, painters, sculptors, musicians) were in some way affected by mental illness—schizophrenia as well as depression or bipolar disorder... The idea of the "mad genius" is so pervasive, there's even a Wikipedia entry for "Creativity and Mental Illness"!

With this novel, I got a chance to explore the idea that creative thought and mental illness are linked. And, yes, I did have to do some research into schizophrenia—symptoms, treatment, etc. But I was writing fiction—so of course my characters and their experiences had to drive the book, not descriptions of the condition. I internalized everything I read, then put it all away. When I drafted (and revised) the novel, I focused on character development, plot, the mother-daughter relationship between Aura and Grace.

AC: *Her mother's condition (and her father's lack of involvement) really hits Aura when she's in middle school, and she feels incapable of assisting her mom—she feels powerless and like she's too young to really help. Do you recall a time when you (as a kid or a teenager) realized the world was bigger, heavier than you thought it was, and that opened your eyes to things, for better or for worse?*

HS: My experience was really the opposite of Aura's: instead of finding that the world was *heavier* than I'd thought, I realized that the world was a lot lighter—by, uh... failing miserably.

The thing is, I'm pretty sure I was the shyest kid in the tri-state area growing up. I know that shyness sounds so incredibly unimportant when you compare it to schizophrenia... But I do remember feeling that the world was a heavy place when I was little—enormous and really just filled with judgment.

I'd always been the classic overachiever. Even if I didn't *like* a course, I studied myself silly. When I started submitting manuscripts, I saw publication as pass or fail: you're either accepted or you're not. So I really felt like I failed for the (gulp) more than seven years it took to get the first acceptance. But I learned that failing really was okay—you have to find out what doesn't work and just keep forging on, right?

AC: *Which of the characters reflects you the most? Who do you wish you resembled (in ability or features or spirit)?*

HS: I think I'm probably most like Aura. I don't mean that we're plagued by the same fears, or that our experiences are the same, but the voice that runs through *A Blue So Dark* sounds an awful lot like me. I think that once I realized how close I still felt to that old teenage me, I just let my natural voice flow straight onto the paper—I wasn't trying to make the book sound *teen*, I was trying to tell a brutally honest story. I think anytime an author writes in first person, though, elements of their own voice are bound to creep in—their own sense of humor, their own observations just can't help but be part of the story when they're using "I."

If I could be *anyone*? When I proofed the novel, I always found myself smiling when Nell entered a scene. There's a real strength about her that I think's fantastic. And there's a straightforwardness about Janny that I really like, too. They're not perfect people—if I've done my job right, *every* character in my book should have their own grab bag of flaws. But I think I wound up surrounding Aura with the kind of people *I* like to be around—real straight shooters.

AC: *If you were aware that your creativity altered or infringed upon your mental state, would you sacrifice your art (your writing, your music, your fine art if you draw like Aura or paint like Aura's mother) to retain your sanity, or would you continue to create?*

HS: No doubt—I'd keep writing. In all honesty, writing is so much a part of who I am anymore, so central to my life, I don't think I'd feel like I had much of a choice.

Take another scenario: let's say I was having trouble breathing, and rushed myself to the ER, and I found out I had this crazy-rare lung disease. And the doctor said, "You're lungs could explode at any minute if you keep breathing." *Huh???* Wait a minute, doc. I'm gonna die if I *don't* breathe. *That's* how I feel about writing—it's just as essential to life as air. And it also pretty much sums up how I'd feel if a psychiatrist told me I had to quit writing or go insane: *I'm gonna go insane if I* don't *write.*

AC: *What else inspires your writing? Do you have a certain routine when you write?*

HS: I'm *constantly* working. Eight (or more) hours a day. Every day.

While that does involve some serious one-on-one time with my computer, I manage to mix it up a bit by doing a lot of outlining in notebooks. I feel *way* too self-conscious writing in public, though. (By "public," I mean a coffeehouse setting, with lots of eyes to watch me... but the edges of the nearby Finley River? Or Lake Springfield? *Fantastic* writing spots ... nobody pays any attention to me there.)

And I always do carry scratch paper with me ... physical activity sort of clears my mind. Out of nowhere (say, while pumping gas or grocery shopping or walking my dog), I get little epiphanies about my characters, or realize how I can fix scenes that have been nagging me. And if I don't write it down, it'll vanish.

AC: *Your artistic abilities extend beyond the printed page. Tell me about your musical endeavors, and how teaching music lessons inspired your writing.*

HS: I've been playing music ever since—well, toddler-dom, if you count pulling out all of Mom's pots and pans and playing the "drums" while she cooked dinner. My first memory is of Mom's piano—I was so small, I'd stand on the floor and stretch my arms up over my head to press the keys!

In all honesty, though, I'm not sure the phrase "musical endeavors" should really be applied to me. Yeah, I love music. And yeah, in college, I did play and sing in a few garage bands ... and I still do write songs, when I have a chance, and am always picking up new instruments to try out (the fiddle, the banjo ... not that I have enough time to practice to do them anything *close* to justice). But I never really pursued music—not like I pursued writing.

I *did*, however, find a way to combine music and writing once I got out of college: by teaching piano and guitar lessons! It was the perfect setup: I'd get up early and write until three in the afternoon, when students would start arriving. That way, I figured, I'd be around literature and music all day... *and* get a few of those pesky bills paid in the process.

At the time, I was drafting adult manuscripts. But after talking to my younger students, I started plowing through drawers and closets, digging out some of my old high school writings... I poured through everything I'd written as a teen: journals, spiral-bound notebooks filled with poetry, class papers, short stories. All those old feelings and experiences came flooding back—and I decided I *had* to try my hand at a YA novel.

Beyond the interaction with my students, though, I think anybody who plays music knows the benefits of repetition—playing the same chord progression or riff over and over until you get it right. The first clumsy time you struggle through "Für Elise" is nothing like the four *hundredth* time you play the piece.

... That's probably why I adore revision so much. The rewrites are truly my favorite part of the process—because that's when a novel (or poem or short story) really starts to *sing*. When all the clumsy fingering's done away with, the sour notes perfected...

AC: A Blue So Dark *is your first published novel, and you have other books sold and in the works as well. What are you currently drafting or polishing?*

HS: I'm *thrilled* to have sold a second YA novel to Flux! *Playing Hurt,* a romance, is set to release in 2011.

Playing Hurt centers on two former athletes: Chelsea Keyes, a basketball star whose promising career has been catastrophically snipped short by a horrific accident on the court, and Clint Morgan, an ex-hockey player who gave up his much-loved sport following his own game-related tragedy.

...I know what you're thinking: *Wait. We go from a literary novel to a romance?* In all honesty, my writing interests are every bit as varied as my reading interests. And I hope that *Playing Hurt* is my first step into writing in *many* different genres.

AC: *What are your ten all-time favorite books?*

HS: Okay—here's the thing. My favorite literature professor in college basically insisted that for a lit student, *good* is an irrelevant term. The books I was studying had *already* been deemed publishable. Had already been deemed classics. As a lit student, it was my job to dig out the meaning, to explore the richness, to figure out, in a sense, why the book *did* get published, *did* become a classic.

...I never unlearned that rule. I still come to a book thinking, *Somebody invested a lot of time and money in pub-*

lishing this book. Somebody thought this was important enough to publish. Why?

So instead of gravitating to specific authors over and over, I'm *constantly* on the lookout for new voices. And instead of really having *favorite* books, I now have favorite tidbits that I take away from *every* novel I read. I always find something to admire. Maybe it's a carefully-crafted plot. Or dialogue that zings. Or gorgeous description. Every published author does something spectacularly well. And the beautiful part is, if you attack books this way, you can help yourself become a better writer every single time you read a new novel...

Allie Costa, known online as Little Willow, runs the blog Bildungsroman. *As a freelance journalist, she writes reviews, reading guides, booklists, articles, and essays. She is also a playwright, a songwriter, and a hopeful novelist. Additionally, she designs and maintains websites for authors and other artists. As an actress, singer, and dancer, she can be found performing when she's not writing or reading. Occasionally, she sleeps. Visit her at http://slayground.livejournal.com.*